LITTLE Love

SIOBHAN SMILE

To the readers who believe Love is Love & it surpasses the parts we are born with.

AUTHOR'S NOTE

This book deals with elements of Age Play (Age Regression) and Domestic Discipline. If you find these subjects to be objectionable then this is not the book for you.

LITTLE LOVE

When the perfect little stumbles into your life, what are you to do?

Lindy Rubin performed every task per her strict routine. She was speeding towards forty and becoming bored with her orderly life. When she began to assess the emptiness of her personal life, she hadn't expected the surprise destined to arrive. Was it fate that brought her a beautiful girl with teary, azure eyes to her doorstep? If so, who was she to deny her Little Love help in her moment of need?

1

LINDY

Lindy Rubin. Public Relations Superstar. I shook my head as I read the most recent article about one of my clients. Something about my personality was perfect for putting out fires. I could make a serial killer look good when I put my mind to it. Closing my phone case, I set it aside and reached for my glass of wine. My gaze searched the room. I took in the details. The body language of the other patrons.

My gift and curse were the ability to size someone up in a matter of a glance. People didn't realize how much they gave away with how they carried themselves—their mannerisms. While that made me plenty of money, it didn't do my personal life any favors. I always seemed to be looking for the clues. It could be as simple as someone crossing their arms. It physically put up a barrier and distance, a defensive posture. Reading my dates usually ended up with them or me not calling again. I was celebrating my thirty-ninth birthday alone as I had most of the milestones and holidays since I left home nineteen years prior.

This year was going to be different, though. I'd decided

to shake up my calm, orderly existence and find myself the baby girl I'd always wanted. Except for a few dates and some casual bed partners I called when the urge struck, I'd never felt any of them could lead to permanence. Occasionally I questioned my ability to feel anything. Emotional attachments seemed too messy. I knew I had to move away from that. I'd caught myself making a to-do list on how to become more spontaneous.

Maybe I was a lost cause. I put on a smile as the server arrived, requested another glass of wine, and went about straightening the items on my table. Once everything was lined up and just right, the server poured more of the red wine into my glass. As soon as I was left to my dinner, I ate slowly. I cut each bite into the perfect size.

A few bites of my steak and roasted vegetables, sip of wine, and use the cloth to wipe the corners of my mouth and repeat. I needed something fresh—someone who wasn't frustrated by my need for control—for my order. My intention was to break the cycle in my personal life. My professional one was demanding of my time and attention. Dates had ended with no second calls after they asked about my work. I was sure that if I formed a connection with someone, my work wouldn't hold as significant of a role. Although, how could I do that after a few hours of conversation over dinner?

To make my insecurities worse, my parents had met at an exclusive private school. They had assured me they'd known they were meant to be. After decades of marriage, my parents were as in love as the day they met. I was jealous of them. I'd never experienced a small fraction of the security they had in their care for each other.

I noticed couples at other tables. They held hands to enjoy their date's presence. Smiles and loving looks shared over a meal. I was the only person there who was alone at a table having dinner instead of sitting at the bar enjoying drinks and conversation with the bartenders. I felt compelled to analyze the interactions. To find the piece that I was missing inside myself.

I cleared my head of everything but my meetings for the next day. Maybe I really was a lost cause. Single wasn't the worst thing. Even though my life was lonely, for the most part, I was happy with that. The few friends I had were as busy with their lives as I was, and aside from sporadic dinners and the occasional weekend getaway, we had our separate things to do.

I finished my dinner, ordered dessert to go, and another glass of wine. It was still early, but I had a lot to prepare for and to make sure my suit was pressed and ready. My lack of femininity also tended to be a point of contention with my dates. As a gender-nonconforming woman, I was vilified for my audacity to break the stereotype of what constituted an acceptable female in society. Although, that was a mental debate for another night.

No matter how much I thought I'd break with my schedules and routine, it always came back to my compulsions for order. I paid my bill and left a tip well above the standard. Back in the day, I worked as a server—not in a fancy restaurant but in a dive bar that served burgers and anything loaded with grease. At times in my life, I realized I felt more content back then even as driven as I was.

I opened the ride app on my phone and requested a car. In half an hour, I'd be home and maybe get an hour to relax before falling asleep in my big, empty bed.

I FLIPPED THROUGH THE CHANNELS WHERE I WAS
seated crossed-legged on my couch. I forced myself not to
stop on every news channel to check in on my clients and if
their fuckery made the news before it came to me. I was
determined to find something fun to watch. My takeout
container of cheesecake sat untouched on the coffee table. I
had on my favorite and well-worn men's pajama set. I tossed
the remote onto the cushion beside me. I was about to
stretch out on the couch when my doorbell echoed through
the house.

When I dropped my feet to the carpet, it started again,
and I frowned as I made my way to the front door. I opened
it and froze when the tiny plump woman with a red, tear-
stained face started yelling at me.

"Asshole, if you didn't want to go on a date with me, all
you had to do was say so. I may not be skinny or all that
pretty, but texting to say you wouldn't show up wouldn't
have cost you anything. You're such an ass, you motherfuc—
Oh." Her bright blue eyes widened to comical size, and she
was frozen on my stoop.

I was caught between confusion and amusement as she
fully focused on me. She was dressed in a cute, pale blue
dress with puffy sleeves, and her curly hair was in a messy
bun. She was adorable. I'd never wanted to cuddle a woman
at first sight as much as I did right then.

"Hello, little love. Bad day?"

"You're not Clarence."

"No, I'm Lindy, I live here."

"Clarence doesn't live here?" She nervously wrung her
hands and looked everywhere, but at me. Even leaning to
the side to glance behind me like the man who stood her up
would suddenly appear.

"No, just me."

"Oh."

"Would you like to come in and wash your face?" I didn't want her to get away. Maybe get her name or some details about her, like where she worked before she escaped back into the night. Fuck, I was sounding like a stalker in my head. Great, another personality quirk that I didn't need to adjust to at almost forty years old.

"No, I should get home, I'm so sorry—"

"Come in. You're not leaving when you're so upset."

I caught her arm as she began to pivot, and I tugged her inside, closing the door and locking it. I spread my hand along her lower back, and my touch seemed to jolt her. She was several inches shorter than my almost six-foot height. I led her to the kitchen at the rear of my home. Then I seated her on one of the barstools along one side of the island. As I put distance between us, I glanced in her direction to find her sitting primly with her hands folded on her lap.

I wanted to touch her. Remove the pins from her bun to see how long the strands were. I busied myself so that I wouldn't make her uncomfortable. I started the kettle for tea, and then wet a rag to wash the tracks of tears from her face. With everything ready, I returned to her and tipped her chin up with my fingertips. I began to gently clean her face of the eye makeup and bright red lipstick.

She stared at me through wide eyes, and I was fascinated with her. Why wasn't she telling me to stop? She'd make the perfect little girl for me. I didn't even know if she was interested in women, or a Domme. But at that moment, I just wanted to care for her. Give her some tea, calm her down, and then call a car to take her home. I'd prefer to tuck her into my guest room bed, but I didn't want to push my luck.

"There, there, little love." I held onto her chin on the

pretense of checking my work, but I just wanted to extend the contact. Imprint the memory of her soft skin and warmth to bring up later on the off chance that I'd never see her again. "Now, who am I making tea for?"

"Katy Campbell."

"Hello, Katy, I'm Lindy Rubin. What would you like in your tea?" I asked as I took the time to throw the washcloth in the laundry room off the kitchen. I quickly made us chamomile tea. She didn't need caffeine this late. By the time I was done, she still hadn't answered. I carried both cups to the island, placed one in front of her, and scooted the sugar cube container toward her.

I added a single cube to mine while I waited for her to get her thoughts together. The wheels were turning in her head. I could almost see her questioning why she was seated in a stranger's kitchen. I wasn't one who allowed someone to disobey me, whether that was at work or in my personal life. I wasn't ashamed of the fact that I craved being in control in every aspect of my existence.

"Is this the address your gentleman friend gave you?"

"Yes, I think. We'd been on a few dates already, and it seemed to be going well. I feel so stupid."

Her eyes turned teary again, and I didn't like that. I wanted to see her smile and hear her laughter. She was the type of woman that deserved to have someone go above and beyond for her.

"For what? Believing you were going go on a third date with someone and then finding out they're, as you put it, an asshole?"

"I thought he liked me."

"His issue, not yours, little love. Feel better with your tea and your pretty face all clean?"

"Yes, thank you. I probably looked crazy showing up on your doorstep."

"Understandable, you were upset. I don't approve of you going to a strange man's home to confront him, but you're not mine. Because of that, I'll refrain from giving you a lecture."

"Lec—lecture?"

"Yes, it was a foolish and dangerous decision. You've been on two dates with the man. Nowhere near enough time to know if he's suitable."

"I thought you weren't going to lecture." She frowned at me.

"If you think that's a lecture then you've never had a proper one before." I slowly sipped at my tea as she seemed to study me. The twin lines between her perfectly arched brows deepening. Her lipstick-stained bottom lip began to pout ever so slightly. "And to be honest, I'm a stranger as well. How do you know I didn't invite you in for some nefarious reasons?"

I suppressed my inclination to show amusement at her apprehensive expression.

"I think I need to go."

She began to slip off the stool, and I held up my hand, and she froze.

"Not until you finish your tea, and I'll get dressed and accompany you home. It's getting late."

"I'll be okay."

"No, you'll wait. Give me ten minutes to change."

I set my cup down and made my way upstairs to my bedroom. Part of me anticipated she'd be gone by the time I returned to her. I changed into jeans and a long-sleeved t-shirt and slipped on my sneakers. On the way out of the room, I grabbed my wallet and keys. I lazily descended the steps. A smile tugged at the corner of my mouth when I found her standing at the sink washing the cups.

"You didn't have to do that."

"I don't mind. You were nice after I showed up like a crazy person on your doorstep."

"As I said, understandable, but don't do that again. It was unsafe. Are you ready? Need to go potty first."

Her face heated, and she shook her head. "Let me put my cheesecake in the fridge, and we'll go." I walked to the living room, turned off the TV, and grabbed the to-go container. When I turned around, she was right on my heels.

"Cheesecake?"

"Yes, from my birthday dinner earlier."

A beautiful smile tilted the corners of her bow-shaped mouth. "Happy birthday."

"Thank you. I don't pay much attention to the day. I just had dinner and came home."

Her happy expression quickly turned concerned at my statement. "That's sad."

"Not really, my friends have families or lives of their own. My parents live in England. My father is a professor and teaching there on a two-year contract, and my mom is doing a lecture series on international relations while there. Would you like it?" I extended the container.

"I couldn't do that. It's your birthday."

"Take it. You'll get more enjoyment out of it than I will."

"Are you saying I'm fat?"

As soon as the question was spoken, I was about to reprimand her until I caught her trying to hide an impish grin. "I don't think I said any such thing. If you're fishing for compliments, I think you're perfect."

"Oh."

"I'm just not one for sweets. It seemed like a good idea when I ordered it to go after dinner. Here." I placed it in her hand.

Once I led her outside, I locked the door. I asked for her address, and then I requested a ride. The night was cooling off. "Did you need a sweater? It's getting cooler out."

"No, I'm fine. You really don't have to go all the way to my place."

"Yes, I do. I want to make sure you get home safely."

She didn't fight me as we waited on the curb, and the app said the car would be there in five minutes. It was now or never. "What is your number?"

"Why?"

"Because I'm going to send you mine, and if you'd ever like to have dinner, I'd love for you to call me."

"Really? Like friends?"

"If that's all you want, of course, if not, more of a date."

"You want to ask me on a date?"

"I believe my intention in getting your number was clear."

Under the streetlight, I saw her face darken with embarrassment. I wanted to order her to call. My dominant side wanted to make sure she'd see me again. Yet I didn't know if that was acceptable. While I assumed she would be perfect as my little, she may be straight and not submissive.

Minutes passed and I remained patient, then she recited her number, and I texted her to make sure she had mine. Her phone pinged just as the car pulled up, and I checked the license plate number.

"Let's get you home." I opened the door and helped her inside. She slid over as I followed her inside. I exchanged a bit of conversation with the driver, telling him I'd be returning home after dropping her off. I felt Katy's attention on me, but she stayed silent. I pressed my thigh up against hers, and she didn't flinch away. I made the decision that if she didn't contact me, I would make the first move.

We pulled up to an older apartment building on the other side of the city. I opened the door and got out. Then I took her hand. "I'll wait until you're inside."

"Thank you, Lindy, it was nice meeting you. Happy birthday."

"Thank you, little love."

It took everything in me to let her go. I waited until the door closed behind her and I got back in the car. On the way home, I saved her number and settled in for the thirty-minute ride. I'd give my little love a few days, and then I'd call her. How could she say no to one date?

2

KATY

It was the lunch rush, and I was running around filling orders for coffee, sandwiches, and whatever else people were demanding now. As if five minutes was too long to wait for their grocery list sized order for a single coffee. My face hurt from all the forced smiles, and I was ready for my shift to end. I loved my job. I was a people person. It was just some days I didn't want to be bothered.

When I was done here, I was off to my second job, which was part-time, and all I had on my schedule was walking dogs for two of my clients. It wasn't bad, and it was exercise. During college, I'd given up on trying to lose weight. Nothing I did short of starving myself would shed more than a few pounds. Yes, I had a FUPA (fat upper pussy area), and my small breasts were starting to head south, but I could live with it. My doctor said I was perfectly healthy—even if I wasn't, starving myself—would be unhealthier than carrying around thirty to fifty pounds too much.

I handed over the large coffee with so much syrup and sugar in it that there was no way it tasted of coffee any longer with a smile and have a nice day. It went that way for another hour until I could breathe, and the co-worker I'd avoided the last two days cornered me.

"I'm sorry, Katy, Clarence always seemed like a nice guy."

I turned away to roll my eyes and removed my apron, collecting my backpack. I powered up my phone and unlocked it. Cecile was nice, and her boyfriend was even nicer. Clarence was one of his best friends. It just proved you never really knew someone.

"You have to say you forgive me."

"There's nothing to forgive. He's the one who stood me up."

Thinking about that night brought up thoughts of Lindy. She appeared older due to her stern, bossy nature, but I couldn't tell. She'd turned out to be nice and understanding after I cussed her out on her front stoop. After she'd made sure I'd gotten home, I'd checked the address and realized I was about three blocks from Clarence's address. I'd felt foolish, my anger had taken over, and I'd acted before thinking. It could've ended much worse.

"No more blind-date setups, I promise."

"I'd appreciate it. I don't really like to date anyway."

The few I'd been on since college had never ended well. Everyone's first impression of me was that I was awkward. Or they interrogated me on why I didn't use my college degree to get a better job. A full and part-time job weren't ideal, but I couldn't see myself putting on dressy clothes every day and going to an office where I'd ended up hating my life. I made good money, but I was saving up for a better place in a safer part of the city. My place was cute, and I'd fixed it up, but the pipes were out of date, and a slight storm would knock the power out.

"Did you call him to find out what happened?"

"No, I went to his place, and it turned out not to be his place. I cussed out the person who lived there before I realized I wasn't talking to Clarence."

"Oh shit. And you didn't need bail money?"

"No, she invited me in for tea and to wash my face." The invite part was a stretch. She hadn't given me much choice. Then she'd washed my face. My shock was intense at her tender caring for me, but for some reason, I liked the way she studied me as she did it. As if I was her sole focus. "She rode with me home to make sure I got there safely. I think she asked me on a date."

"Think?" she asked and waited for me to answer.

I almost smiled at her excess energy starting to build. I could tell from the way she started bouncing on her toes. She was one of those women who could've been a supermodel if she had about another six inches on her height.

"Well, she asked for my number and said if I wanted to have dinner to call her."

"What did you say?" Her frustration was clear in her tone as she made me feel like she was having to pull teeth to get the information she wanted.

"I just gave her my number. I mean a woman's never hit on me or at least I don't think so. I'm clueless about those types of things. She lived in a really nice brownstone in the most exclusive neighborhood in Ivy Harbor. She was older, or I think she was older. I was too confused to think. I went from furious to just wrung-out."

"Well, are you going to call her?"

"I don't know. What am I supposed to say? She probably thinks I'm crazy. She lectured me on my unsafe decision to go to some man's home."

"I think you should call her. What's the worst that could

happen? A nice meal. Conversation. Maybe some mutual orgasms."

"I don't sleep with people on the first date." Well, there had been that phase in college where weekends were for hookups, but it had always been guys from my class and that one professor that I ended up mentally writing my paper for his class as he pounded away. I should've gotten an *Oscar* for that performance.

"Either way, I think you should go for it. Maybe it was fate or something that had you show up at her house."

"You think? She seemed so confident and put-together." I sighed as I removed the tie from my hair. "Everyone wants to know why I'm not putting my MBA to use or I'm being asked don't I want—"

"Stop right there, you showed up on this woman's doorstep looking a mess and cussing, and she still wanted to go out with you. Maybe it's not even that kinda dinner. It could be just a friend dinner."

"What if I'm curious about more than a friend dinner? Women are conditioned to compare themselves to other women. We...I don't know. I thought she was beautiful and, well, I kinda liked the way she took care of me. She washed my face. Made me tea. I wasn't even upset about the lecture."

"Then I think you should go for it. One date can't hurt, right? You might even find you want a second date. People are so hung up on gender and all that bullshit. Lots of people don't realize they're bisexual until they meet the one. Take the chance."

"I might. After I'm done with my dog walking clients, I'll call. Maybe I can figure out if she meant a friend date or something more."

"Good for you. And again, I'm sorry about that Clarence

asshole, Jonnie took care of it. He made sure Clarence knew he was a fucker for pulling that childish shit."

"He didn't have to do that, but thank him for me."

"Will do. Now, go take care of what you need to and then call her. What's her name?"

"Lindy, Lindy Rubin."

"I know that name."

She grabbed my phone and opened the browser, tapped on the screen, and then her eyes widened. Was Lindy married? A serial killer?

"What? What's wrong?"

"Society page says...Public relations powerhouse, Lindy Rubin is making quite a name for herself in the upper-class society of Ivy Harbor. Her name is connected to senators and billionaires. But rumor has it that she's single. At last nights' ten-grand a plate charity dinner for the Roth Foundation, she was seen arriving alone. Our reporters there that night were unable to get a comment."

I really wished she hadn't read that. I didn't spend ten thousand a year in rent and bills, that was half of what I made in a year.

"Wow, she's...if you don't go for it, I will. Successful, beautiful, and fills out a suit quite sinfully."

She handed me my phone back, and I stared at the screen. The tuxedo Lindy had worn screamed designer label. She was slim and elegant. The smile she wore was fake. It didn't crinkle the corners of her eyes like the ones she'd given me the other night.

"Now, I'm not so confident about this."

"No, I didn't mean to make you insecure, but you know she's not some insane person. Society page said she was single. Go for it. One date, promise me you'll call for at least that."

"I promise. But if I make a fool of myself, you can hear me bitch about it all day tomorrow."

"Deal."

I said my goodbyes, grabbed a large coffee with just cream and sugar, and one of the sandwiches from the case. Our bosses provided two meals a day when you worked that you could get any time during your shift. I exited the shop and turned right. My first pickup was only a fifteen-minute walk away, then another block for the other, and afterward was straight to the dog park for an hour to let them run off their energy.

My brain started to form all the reasons not to call, but like Cecile said, what's the worst thing that could happen?

I WAS TIRED AND READY TO SHOWER AND JUST RELAX IN front of the TV for a few hours before bedtime. I had the opening shift the next day. That meant I needed to be there at five AM. The owner would be finishing up baking since they started their day at two AM. The sandwich had held me over, but I'd heat some soup while I made the call. As much as I'd assured myself that it was only a conversation, I was still nervous.

I kicked off my shoes inside my bedroom door and headed for the kitchen. I unlocked my phone and searched for the text that just said Lindy. Before I could chicken out, I connected the call.

Nervously I nibbled on my bottom lip and busied myself as it rang. I was about to give up when a soft, husky voice answered.

"Hello, little love, I was wondering if I was going to need to call you."

"Sorry, I was debating. I didn't make a good impression."

I cringed as I realized what I said. Being indecisive with a woman like Lindy probably wasn't any better than me crying and raging at her door. Although, something in my gut made me want to be honest about my self-consciousness about calling her.

"You made all the impression you needed. Have you been behaving? No visiting strange men's homes in the middle of the night."

My lips quirked at the corners as I noticed the amusement in her voice.

"I don't think ten PM constitutes middle of the night, but no, I haven't made any more visits."

"Good girl." Her voice dipped lower, and it did strange things to my belly. "Were you calling to take me up on the offer of dinner?"

"I'm a little unsure of why you want to take me to dinner."

"You're beautiful and adorable, and I'm hoping at least bisexual."

That surprised a laugh out of me, and I snorted. "I don't know, I've never gone on a date with a woman before. My friend told me I should just go for it."

"And I heartily agree with her. I have a business dinner Friday night, but what if I pick you up on Saturday?"

"I think that would be okay. What time?"

"How about seven? I'll make reservations somewhere."

"Sounds great."

"How was your day?

Her unexpected question made me hesitate. I assumed we'd settle on a time and hang up, but I was secretly excited she wasn't ready to end the conversation. "It was okay. I'm a barista at The Light Coffeehouse. I worked there until three, and then I walked a few dogs for my clients."

"Two jobs?"

"Yes, but only one full-time one. The dog walking job started as a way to make extra cash during college. I just didn't give up some of my clients when I graduated." I felt the need to defend my choices. I'd done it so many times it was second nature.

"As long as it's something you enjoy."

There was no judgment or further questioning as to what I went to college for or why was I just a lowly barista. "My friend searched your name."

"And?"

I frowned as a bit of coldness settled into her tone.

"Do you like your job?"

"It has its moments. I'm good at it, and for the most part, I enjoy it. I won't say that I don't have clients that I'm not fond of, but morally I have no complaints. They're just...entitled."

"You were on the society page."

She chuckled and the tension I felt eased at having possibly overstepped.

"They're more interested in my supposed wealth and bed partners than anything else. I'm always ready with a no comment."

"I should go. I just got home. I need to shower and make something to eat. I open in the morning."

"Well, get plenty of rest, and don't hesitate to call before our date or send me a text. Nothing says we can't share conversations before a first date."

"True. I'm looking forward to Saturday."

"I am too. I was going to contact you tomorrow if I hadn't heard from you."

Some of my lingering insecurity about going out with the beautiful, successful woman faded away. I just couldn't put my finger on what intrigued me so much about her. I'd seen plenty of beautiful women, people, and a lot of them were powerful. None of them made me think about a first kiss at the end of a date before. Would she be as commanding in every aspect of her life? Whatever was going on with me settled into my lower belly. It was nerves and something else, and that something else frightened me a bit.

"I'm glad I called then. Um, goodnight."

"Goodnight, little love. Get plenty of rest, and I'll see you Saturday at seven."

I disconnected the call with what I was sure looked like a goofy grin and was glad I lived alone. It hit me like a sledgehammer to the gut when I realized I was going to need to buy something to wear. Would she take me someplace fancy? Would we split the bill? My budget was fast-food level—value menu. I forced myself to calm down, and I'd text or call to see where she was taking me. I could freak out later about clothes and everything else.

3

LINDY

My reflection stared back at me as I studied myself. I straightened my tie and turned to the side, left then right. It had been a long time since I had a date that wasn't conducted with the propriety of a business dinner, and I didn't want to view her in that way. I slipped my feet into my stilettos and picked up my dove-colored suit jacket from where I'd hung it on the hook beside the mirror. Part of me was hoping that this would end well, and my prospective little girl would be interested in seeing me again.

I couldn't remember the last time I looked forward to a date. Hookups were easy to come by. Five minutes in a bar and you could go home with anyone as long as you properly played the game, or at the very least, a swipe in a dating app. Yet, this wasn't a hookup. It wouldn't end in a hotel room or with an early morning car ride home. One date, but my brain couldn't shut off what I was truly worried about. To me, a Mommy Domme/little relationship wasn't about sex. It was care and discipline, someone's gift of unwavering trust. That was different from the dominance I showed in the bedroom. Domestic discipline hadn't meshed with the few women I'd brought the idea up with.

It wasn't something I needed to get off, but I had to admit I was more content in a relationship where I had a submissive. Play was different. I wanted things to work out with her and have it mean more than a scene to be played out before we parted ways. Now I just needed to make a good impression during our date.

I slipped my hand in my pocket and retrieved my pocket watch and checked the time. It was something people found odd, but as much as I was attached to my phone for work, in my private life, I wasn't one to stare at my phone. The time said I needed to meet my driver outside. Usually, I just grabbed a car from a rideshare app, but I'd arranged to have my usual driver that I used for business to drive us.

The day after she'd agreed to have dinner with me, she'd sent me a message asking where I was taking her. I sensed that my supposed wealth bothered her, so I'd chosen a restaurant she'd be more comfortable going to. I'd assured her I was paying for dinner and anything else on our date. I was a bit old-fashioned in that regard. When I requested a date, I picked them up, opened the door, and paid the bill. Then at the end, I would walk them to their door. It was part of my dominant nature—my showing I cared for them and their well-being beyond their willingness to fuck.

From the conversations and messages that we'd shared in the past few days, I knew she was independent. She had plans and was determined to take care of herself. I wouldn't take that from her, but we'd need to have a conversation if this continued into a relationship.

I slipped on my jacket and placed my wallet in the inner pocket. The suit was perfectly tailored and timeless. I wore the occasional dress if the opportunity called for it. I was a *Butch* from birth. I preferred my hair long to keep it in a bun. It annoyed me if it touched my face.

I descended the stairs to the second level and lower to the first floor and made sure everything was closed and locked. I exited after removing the bouquet of wildflowers from the fridge. She didn't seem the roses type. She was colorful and free-spirited, even if she thought she appeared awkward.

The driver opened the door, and I got in the back of the limo. I'd given him the itinerary for the evening earlier when he'd dropped me off after work. It was dinner, then dancing at a blues club that a friend of mine owned. She'd promised to reserve me a private table in a corner. Then it was Katy's choice whether she wanted the evening to end. Maybe dessert and a walk. I was confident I wouldn't complain about spending a bit more time with her.

The door closed, and I placed the flowers on the seat next to me. I was strangely nervous. My parents had raised me to be self-assured and unapologetic about my life or how I chose to live it. I knew they supported me in whatever I did, even though I was sure they were disappointed that I wasn't settled down yet. They told me that it would happen when I was ready.

The partition lowered, and Gary informed me we were pulling up outside.

"I'll get the door for her."

"Sure thing. Show is all yours, Lindy."

I thanked him. He'd been with me for four years since my private firm had taken off, and I was suddenly in the society section every week. I opened the door and discovered he'd found a spot big enough for the car at the curb. Straightening my jacket, I made my way inside holding the flowers. It was a rundown walkup building. I wasn't happy with the accommodations, but it wasn't my place to say something...yet.

I paused outside her door on the third floor and heard scuffling and cursing on the other side. When she answered, she was smoothing her curls she had in an up-do, and a few framed her face. I approved of her light makeup and the pale pink of her lipstick. She wore a beautiful, sheath dress in dark crimson that made her pale skin look even creamier. A cute spattering of cinnamon-colored freckles dusted her shoulders exposed by the narrow straps.

"You're right on time, and I'm still—"

"Take your time."

"Please come in." She motioned for me to enter, and the lock clicked softly behind me.

I handed her the flowers and loved the way she brightened when she smiled.

"Thank you. They're beautiful. I think I have a vase. Would you like something to drink?"

"You're welcome, and no, I'm fine, thank you."

While she searched for a vase in her kitchen cabinets, I studied her apartment. It was a small, one-bedroom, close in size to the place I lived in during college. It was cute, with fresh paint and vintage scuffed hardwood floors. She seemed to love the color blue—every shade of it was in her furniture and decorations.

"I just need to put on shoes. I went shopping and couldn't decide what to wear, and I got behind and—"

I stopped her by circling her upper arm. Her skin was

silky and warm, and she had the faintest hint of some spicy perfume.

"You look beautiful. I want you to stop being nervous. We're going to dinner and dancing, then maybe a walk for some more conversation. You will relax, and we'll enjoy each other's company. Understood?" I kept my voice low with just a hint of command as I kept eye contact.

"Yes, sorry."

I lowered my mouth to hers and brushed a light kiss to the corner of her mouth. "No need to apologize. The car is ready, and we still have time before our reservation." I stroked her arm with my thumb before releasing her. "Now, get your shoes on and make sure you have everything."

She nodded and took off barefoot, running to what I assumed was her bedroom. She returned a few minutes later, and I helped her with the silk wrap that matched her dress. As was my habit, I led her downstairs with my hand on her lower back, opened the door, and assisted her inside. I could tell from her shy blushes and glances that she wasn't used to the treatment. We spoke easily, nothing too in-depth and the roundness of her hip pressed to mine distracted me. She seemed to lean into my side unconsciously, but stiffened when she caught herself.

When we arrived, I told Gary that I would call him when we were done. We were early, but our table was ready. I'd requested a private table in a quiet corner. We ordered drinks, but I put off looking at the menu.

"This is a nice place."

"It is. It's one of my favorites. I think I've tried just about everything on the menu. What did you do today?"

"It's my weekend off in the rotation, so I took care of a couple of my clients for the part-time job and then went shopping. I forgot to say that you look great."

"Thank you. I was unsure of what to wear myself. I don't date all that much. Scheduling wise, I'm always working. I made sure to rearrange everything so you could have my full attention tonight."

"You must work a lot."

"It tends to be an around the clock job. Drama doesn't wait for nine-to-five hours."

"Why did you get into public relations?"

"I don't know. I sort of fell into it after I finished school. I found that I was good at it, and then it turned into a career."

"What about your parents?"

"My parents are professors. They travel around to teach about political science and international relations. My mother was briefly an ambassador but found that it kept her away from home too much. My parents tend to be attached at the hip. Where one is the other isn't far away."

"Sounds like a fun way to grow up."

"It had its moments. The moving around was the hardest part. I was always the new kid in whatever private or boarding school they enrolled me in. Being out as a lesbian from an early age also didn't make me many friends. Some places we lived weren't queer-friendly. What about your parents?"

"Dad is a foreman on an oil rig in the middle of the ocean, and my mom is a schoolteacher, home was always Texas. They've been married since they graduated from high school. Went from graduation ceremony to the justice of the peace. Dad enlisted in the Marines and wanted his ring on Mom's finger before he left for bootcamp. He claimed he didn't want any other men sniffing around his girl while he was away."

"I would sympathize."

I watched her face brighten more as she spoke of her

parents and growing up. She mentioned her MBA and how people thought she should be doing more with her life. Time passed too quickly as I sat there enjoying the cheerfulness in her voice. She was animated and spoke with her hands, and she leaned in when she talked. Her body language was open, and she was relaxed.

"Our lives aren't for others to choose for us. Maybe one day you'll use your degree, but only when you're ready."

"Thanks, I don't like to mention other dates when I'm on one, but they always questioned me on why I was just a barista. It's a good job. Sometimes the tips are amazing. I'm thirty-two. I have plenty of time. I'll so-called adult when I'm ready."

"Of course you will. Ready to order dinner?"

"Yes, I didn't mean to talk your ear off."

"I asked for your story. I didn't put a limit on the time you could talk about it. How will I get to know you if we don't share? Also, your family makes you happy."

We ordered and continued talking through dinner and a few drinks, until it was time to move to the next phase of our date.

***

THE SPOTLIGHT LOUNGE WAS A LITTLE HOLE IN THE wall place, but it was a staple of Ivy Harbor. It had survived for nearly fifty years. The band played smooth jazz and blues. I noticed the few drinks over dinner, and the one she was currently nursing, had turned her cheeks pink. She wasn't a drinker. I wasn't one myself, so I approved.

A slow song began. I stood, held out my hand, and she took it without argument. I led her to the small dance floor. I heard her gasp as I pulled her to me. Her soft curves conformed to my angles, and it was perfect. From our talks and things that she'd said, I was the first woman she'd gone out with. Her hands shook slightly where her right rested on my shoulder, and I held her left.

She followed beautifully as I moved us to the music. She looked up at me from under thick, dark lashes. The unfamiliarity of her attraction was palatable. She wanted me, yet didn't understand why. I urged her closer by flexing my arm and applying slightly more pressure to her lower back. Her breasts were small, disproportionate for her plump frame, but I loved her shape. How her hips flared and made her waist appear tinier.

I urged myself to remember this was a first date. She wasn't someone to be played with lightly. I also knew that leaving her at her door later would be the hardest thing I'd ever done. I moved her left hand to my shoulder and spread both hands over her back, my little fingers riding the curve where her plump cheeks swelled beneath the skirt of her dress.

I don't know how many songs played or how long we danced, but the more time passed, the more she melted into my taller, slimmer frame. I wanted more than the chaste kiss I'd given her in her apartment. But also knew before I took her to bed, I needed her to have no doubts about her attraction or what I would demand of her.

Everything in me said she was mine. I wanted to believe it. To trust that what I felt wasn't a momentary lapse. I craved a second, third, hundredth date, mutual affection and need, and her complete trust and submission. We liked to believe that happily-ever-afters were forever, but sometimes unlike in those romance novels my mother devoured, all we could expect was a happily for now. A few months or years, before the heat waned.

I was greedy and required everything. I kept silent—swore I wouldn't confess too early. The beautiful little girl in my arms wasn't the one-night-stand type—she'd believe in the fairy tales. I wanted to give her those, but I knew she needed more time. Trust didn't happen over a few days of conversation, at least not the trust I demanded.

THREE HOURS LATER, WE STOOD OUTSIDE HER DOOR. "Goodnight, little love." I don't know what came over me, but I stepped closer even as I told myself to keep my distance.

The way she focused on my lips said she wanted me to kiss her. I could practically feel the warmth of her hands almost touching my sides. She seemed almost frightened of her need. I put both of us out of our misery. I'd wanted to kiss her all night.

I gripped the back of her dress, wrapping it in my fists. I teased her, licked at the seam of her soft lips, and tugged her closer. My brain and body warred with the call for instant gratification or a slow claiming. I could seduce her. Make her incapable of saying no. This was new for her and probably overwhelming. I separated our lips only a breath apart.

"Get some rest, baby girl. I'll call you tomorrow." I nipped at her bottom lip and savored her sexy gasp. "And if you're missing me just a little"—I made a show of getting my business card that I'd written all my information on earlier—"my address is on the back. Also, if you can't get me on my cell, call my office number."

As if on auto-pilot, she took my card and spun. With her back to me, I wanted to touch her just one more time. I placed my hand on the pliant curve of her belly and squeezed. My fingers sank into her flesh, and I almost said fuck my plan as I jerked her back against me.

She got her door open and stumbled inside. I chuckled as the door slammed, and I loved how off-balance I made her. I'd give her a few days to think, then I was coming for her and we'd make plans for date number two.

4

KATY

"**G**oodnight, little love." Her gaze bore into mine as her body seemed to crowd mine against my apartment door.

I couldn't keep my focus off her mouth. Her lips were dark pink and lipstick free. I'd never wanted a kiss more in my life, but I couldn't force myself to make the first move. My hands hovered at her sides. She was smirking down at me, and then it happened—she kissed me.

She groaned, and her hands fisted in the fabric at my lower back. My body arched into hers. She was warm, solid, yet, soft. I lifted onto my toes to get closer. Her tongue gently stroked along the seam of my lips. Just as I wrapped my arms around her neck, she pulled back. I tightened my thighs, and my nipples pushed to the padding of my bra.

"Get some rest, baby girl. I'll call you tomorrow."

She nipped at my bottom lip, and I sighed as she slipped from my arms.

"And if you're missing me just a little"—she reached into her jacket and pulled out a card—"my address is on the back. Also, if you can't get me on my cell, call my office number."

I took the card, turned around, and unlocked my door. I was caught between a trembling mess and frozen to the floor as her slim hand spread over my belly. She gave it a gentle squeeze, and I nearly fell into my apartment. I stuttered out a goodnight and practically slammed the door.

Embarrassment still stung my cheeks. All I could remember was rethinking the end of our date. Was I too needy? Did I not kiss her right? Was kissing a woman different than a man? She hadn't called, and I tried to remember her life was busy. Every time I tried to send her a message or call her, I froze up. It was the normal end of the date thing, a kiss to say goodbye or thanks.

"What is with you today?" Cecile asked me during a slow period. "You've been distracted since your date. You won't even give me details."

"She kissed me, and I don't know, I freaked out afterward." I couldn't get over the way she'd gripped my stomach, and she'd pressed completely to me. Was it strange that she was the first person to ever just hold onto my belly? It had grown softer and rounder over the years. It was the one part of myself I was most self-conscious about. Everyone had that one thing they'd change if they were offered the option.

"Did she try anything else?"

"No, just kissed me and said goodnight, made sure I had her card with her address and work number on it. I just keep thinking I was too needy or something."

"I think if that was the case, she wouldn't have given you her info. And secondly, if it was me, I'd want the person I was interested in to know we were on the same page. Call her. Don't let your insecurity over something different make you lose out on this."

"I'd take her advice."

I spun to find Lindy standing on the other side of the counter. She looked elegant, but her smile was wicked, or I thought it was. I seemed to have sex on the brain a lot since I met her.

"What are you doing here?"

"Well, I had a meeting a few blocks away and thought since my little love hadn't called me back, I'd stop in to check on you. I was just lucky that you were working."

"Can I get you a coffee or something?" I asked, trying to buy time.

"A large coffee, black, and maybe a few minutes to talk?"

"She has a few minutes. I'll make your coffee." I shook my head as my supposed friend pushed me out from behind the counter.

"Lindy, this is Cecile." I gave a quick introduction.

"A pleasure to meet you, Cecile. I think I owe you a thank you for talking her into going out with me."

"You're welcome."

She handed Lindy the large to-go cup and shooed up both away. I led her out front and around the corner to the mouth of the alley.

"If I did something inappropriate or something you didn't like, you tell me. This doesn't work without complete honesty."

I'd expected more lead up, but then I realized she wasn't the type. She was direct. I found that to be a big part of her charm. She'd been open and honest, answered every question, and asked as many about me. I don't remember a time I was on a date that it felt almost even, or they were interested in every detail of my likes and dislikes. When she'd danced with me, she was completely present.

"I was embarrassed about how I reacted and if—"

"It was a first date kiss. I don't typically stay over on the first night unless it's a hook-up. It was hard to walk away, but I want a second date. Yet I don't want you to think that I only want to get you in bed. That will happen at a later date."

I choked out a laugh and started to back up as she approached. She placed her hand on the wall over my shoulder. I looked around to make sure no one was watching.

"No one can see us."

Her tone was soothing, but I felt guilty over it. It wasn't anyone's business who I dated or was interested in.

"I'm sorry."

"We're going to need to have a serious conversation. Just because I was safe and secure enough growing up to never know the inside of a closet. I wouldn't even pretend to understand what it's like to develop an attraction to a woman and find myself questioning everything. One day, if this works out, you'll be the next big thing on the society page."

"No, don't threaten me with that."

"I can't guarantee that it won't happen. You're going to have to be prepared. If this becomes serious, which I hope it does, I won't keep you a secret, but I'll protect your privacy as long as I can."

I nodded and knew she'd go above and beyond until I was comfortable. I liked the fact she overlooked my awkwardness—that it wasn't a deal-breaker. I raised my hands and tugged at her tie, rubbing the silk between my fingertips and thumbs.

"I want you to come over tonight, I'll make you dinner, and we can talk. Just the two of us."

Just the two of us, I wondered if that meant more kisses I wouldn't freak out about afterward.

"What time?"

"I canceled a meeting on the chance I could talk you into coming over, so I'll be home around six."

"I finish here at three. Then I'll go home, shower, and come by."

"Sounds good. Get back to work before I try to talk you into taking off early."

"Unfortunately, I can't leave Cecile alone."

"Are you tempted, though?"

She smirked and slowly lowered her mouth to mine. When she hesitated, her breath teased my lips, and I sunk my teeth in the lower curve as I waited to see what she'd do.

"Maybe."

"You're a tease, little love."

She gave me a quick, playful kiss and backed away from me. She reminded me of what time to be at her place, and I watched her until she disappeared into the back of her limo. I stood there for a few minutes getting myself together and went back inside.

"So, still together or—"

"We're having dinner at her place tonight after she gets off work."

"Good. From the few minutes I spoke with her, I think she's perfect for you. And she's way hotter in person."

I didn't have to answer because the afternoon rush started, and we were busy until my replacement showed up when it was time for me to leave. I mentally picked out the dress that I wanted to wear. Hanging out at her place should probably be casual, but I still wanted to be pretty. I had plenty of sundresses that I hadn't put away yet for the approaching winter.

Instead of walking home like I normally would have, I requested a car and arrived home a half-hour early. As soon as I was inside, I ran for the bathroom stripping and wondering should I shave above the knee. Did I need to trim or wax? Then I realized I was thinking of changing myself. I wanted her to like me for me without all the shit I did in the past for the men. The waxing and the primping, the body shapers, and everything else to make the lumps and bumps disappear. During the dance and the kiss, she'd felt it all, and she'd still came to ask me out again.

I laughed at myself getting stupid for a minute and calmed down. It was a second date, so nothing was going to happen. It was just dinner and hanging out because she wouldn't push until I was ready. For now, I was okay with the kisses and flirting. I didn't know about the rest yet. Curious, but scared.

I took a quick shower, dried off, and went to my bedroom. I stood in front of my tiny packed closet and went through each dress, the one I thought about was a no, so I went through ten more until I found the one that I wanted. It was pink with tiny white flowers and puffy sleeves, and it hung to mid-thigh. I picked a pair of plain, white bikini panties and decided against a bra.

After I was dressed, I was too early, but I wanted to get something to take, which meant a stop at the store. I wasn't a drinker, so I decided against wine or beer. I didn't know anything about pairings or stuff like that. I could handle picking dessert. To kill a bit of time, I straightened up my place. Trying to pretend I wasn't a little nervous was making me more apprehensive.

How the hell did I make it to thirty-two without having a complete nervous breakdown? I guess it wasn't too late to meltdown, and this would be the time to do it.

I SHOWED UP FIVE MINUTES EARLY, WITH A CHOCOLATE-covered strawberry cheesecake, which I hadn't been able to resist. If she didn't like it, I could eat it all myself. I rang the doorbell and waited. A smile curved my lips as the door opened to expose Lindy's leanly muscled frame in jeans and a men's tank. I was shocked to find tattoos covering her chest down to mid-forearm. Monochrome designs of gothic horror scenes, including vampires, Lycan, and all manner of creatures and gore.

"I think that's a deal-breaker."

"Too bad, little love, get your ass in here. I'm a little behind. I got stuck on a last-minute call. Dinner is going to take a few minutes longer than anticipated."

I let her tug me inside, and I strode back to the kitchen as I heard the door close, the heavy lock clicked into place. I didn't even ask as I opened the fridge and slid the bakery box onto the bottom shelf, pushing a few things out of the way to make room.

"While you're in there, grab the iced tea for me, baby girl."

"Is it still okay that you took the night off?" I asked as I did what she asked. She pointed to the empty glass with ice and the half-full one, so I filled them with tea.

"Nothing that won't wait until morning. It just means I need to go in an hour earlier than normal. And before I appear rude, you look beautiful as always."

"Thank you. I was nervous about what to wear."

"No reason to be. You don't have to dress fancy in my home. I should have said casual when I invited you over. Could you bring me the pasta on the cutting board right there?"

I picked up the flexible sheet with thin noodles. "You make your own?"

"Is there any other way?"

I don't even know if I'd had real pasta that wasn't dried and came in a box for a buck from the grocery store. "Um, well, there's a whole aisle of pasta already done and ready—"

I loved the richness of her laughter and caught her shaking her head at me. "I feel my efforts on this dinner are going to be unappreciated."

I laughed as I stepped up beside her to find a pan with sauce that didn't look like it came from a jar.

"You cooked everything from scratch?"

She dropped the pasta in boiling water and handed me the sheet back. I carried it to the open dishwasher and placed it inside. I hadn't helped with a meal since I was kid and Mom asked me to. Because of how I'd met her and what I'd learned, I'd assumed I'd show up to takeout containers and her dressed in her usual dress shirt and tie, maybe one just not as fancy as the expensive linen ones she'd worn on our date and earlier.

"I tend to eat out a lot, but this seemed special. I broke out my rusty kitchen skills just for you."

"I'm feeling special, and I'm sorry. I'll try to be more...appreciative."

"You can show your appreciation when we cuddle later and watch a movie."

"Oh." Thought of cuddling with her made my heart kick into a faster pace, and that weird feeling in my lower tummy was back in full force. I didn't want to think this was about sex or my long-ignored libido, but what if it was? What if my body just wanted to be loved on, and it didn't care about who that was? Using her to get off and nothing else seemed...wrong to me.

"Relax, cuddle, nothing else. We'll both be keeping our clothes on...tonight. Now, have a seat while I finish dinner."

I slid onto a barstool, leaned my forearms on the island surface, and curled my hands around the perspiring glass. She was confident, and her movements precise, not one wasted.

"What are you thinking?"

"Why am I here?"

"Because I want you here. But the real question is, do you want to be here?"

"I like you. I mean, I'm still processing. This is odd to me, and it's not all because you're a woman." I kept the strength of my sexual attraction to myself for the time being.

"You have all the time you need. Dinner is ready."

I started to get up to make a plate.

"No, baby girl, you'll sit there, and I'll feed you. That is not up for debate. When we're in this house, I take care of you. Is that agreeable?"

No matter if it was phrased as a question, it was nothing more than an order. She was in no way asking if I agreed.

"Yes, ma'am."

"That's a good girl."

The rest of the evening went the same way. I wasn't allowed to lift a finger unless she asked for my help. She fed me more than I did myself, which included dinner and dessert. After she'd scrubbed the kitchen, she led me into the living room. I didn't fight her when she pulled me down on the couch and shifted me until I was almost sitting on her lap. She tucked my head under her chin, and I relaxed as she turned on the TV.

I could definitely get used to this.

5

LINDY

A month of late-night phone calls, text messages throughout the day, and not enough dates, and I was ready to move onto the serious part of our relationship. Unfortunately, my clients weren't allowing me to seduce my little love as much as I wanted. I'd had to cancel dates and exchanged dinners for lunches. She'd only come to my house that one night and that had been the last time we were alone.

That's why I'd spent a week rearranging my schedule so that we'd have a weekend to ourselves. I'd even made reservations if she were open to getting out of town for a couple of days. I knew this was her weekend off. I'd called her from the office at lunchtime to double-check when she would be home, and I was planning to kidnap her—even if that was just to my house for a few days.

I jogged up the steps to her apartment and knocked on the door. I shoved my hands in my pockets and waited for her to answer. When the door opened, I smiled to find her in a tight t-shirt and sleep shorts that rode the top of her thick thighs. The hard tips of her breasts made it obvious she wasn't wearing a bra beneath her thin shirt.

"I should come over unannounced more often."

"What are you doing here?"

"I was wondering what you'd say to two days in a very nice hotel on the beach or at the very least at my place?"

"A weekend away? But what about work?"

"I called in a friend at my old firm who owed me a couple favors, and he's gonna man my office for the weekend to take care of any emergencies. I don't have to be back at work until eight AM Monday morning. My job sucks for relationships, but until you, I didn't have the urge to move everything around to get time. What do you say you pack a bag, maybe a skimpy bikini and make it worth my while?"

"You'll have to buy me one of those."

"Get to packing, little love. You're all mine for the next two days."

She squealed as she gave me a quick hug and then took off running. I entered and closed the door behind me. I waited in the living room, catching glimpses of her quickly packing. I groaned as she pushed her shorts down, exposing fat cheeks and perfect dimpled thighs. I'd spent a month fantasizing about that plump form in my bed. Now I had two days to make her mine, but first the talk. While I'd taken care of her, we hadn't discussed what that meant or the fact she'd have rules, and her every need would be taken care of by me.

As far as I knew, she wasn't familiar with the lifestyle. Daddy Doms were a lot more prevalent than Mommy ones, but the care and discipline were no different.

"Where are we going?" She emerged wearing jeans and a t-shirt, an overnight bag in her right hand.

"Well, tonight it's back to my place, and we leave early tomorrow. It's about a three-hour drive. Tonight, we'll order some takeout, then this weekend, we'll take advantage of a beach and room service."

"You won't get any complaints from me."

"I didn't think I would."

"You didn't have to go to the trouble. I know how demanding your job is. I can't imagine the nightmare it was to get even a few days off."

"But I have something more important than my job now. So let me spoil you for a weekend before I have to sell my soul again for another weekend."

"I'm yours to spoil."

"You better be. I rented a car for the drive. We're all good to go."

We made sure everything was turned off and locked, and then I held her hand as we descended the stairs. Once we were at the car, I opened the passenger door, and when she sat down, I crouched and buckled her in. Made sure she was safe. I stroked my hand over her belly, teased the adorable rolls beneath her t-shirt. My other hand curved around the back of her head and tugged her mouth to mine.

"We're sharing a bed this weekend. If that's not something you want, you have to tell me. But first, when we get home, we need to have a serious talk. It's nothing bad, but it's important."

I pressed my lips to hers, savored the way they conformed to mine, and I didn't hold back. A little moan slipped out, and I deepened the kiss until I made myself back away.

"We'll finish that when we get home."

She nodded shyly, and I straightened and closed the door. I walked to the front and waited for traffic to pass.

Then I started the short trip to my place. I found her staring out the window and wondered if I'd scared her with the talk comment. I just needed to get everything out. Hiding a part of myself from her didn't sit right with me. I'd never held back before.

I'd demanded us be honest with each other, and I'd been keeping a secret. It was too much like lying to me. I pulled into the empty parking spot outside my home. I ushered her inside, showed her to my room, and dropped off her bag. She didn't protest. I took that as an agreement to sharing my bed. She told me she was going to change back into her pajamas and disappeared into the master bathroom. I almost protested because I wanted to bathe her, but again we needed to talk.

Before long, I had her seated on the counter with her going through takeout menus. I stepped up in front of her, placed my hands on her knees, and gently pushed them apart. I slipped between her thighs, and her legs gripped my waist.

"Anything looking good?"

"Well..." She set the menus aside and draped her arms over my shoulders.

"Now, now, baby girl, once you have a full belly, then you get a reward. Don't think I didn't notice you changed clothes, exposing your pretty body. Naughty baby girls get spanked for that."

I pushed my hands under her t-shirt and roughly pinched her thick nipples, rolling the distended peaks. When she shivered and arched, I increased the pressure to the point of pain and then removed my touch completely.

"Before you get yourself played with, you're going to learn a few things about me. Do you know what a Domme is?"

Her gaze locked on mine, and she nodded.

"Well, I assume you know what a Daddy Dom is?"

"They liked to be in control and have someone call them Daddy."

"Basically, yes. But Daddy and Mommy Doms take care of their babies and littles. We like to care for our littles in every way, make sure they're happy and safe, but also correct them when needed."

"You-you're saying you want to be my Mommy Domme? Is that why you always call me little love or baby girl?"

"Yes, but being my little has nothing to do with sex unless that's what we want. But also I want to be your Domme, and you be my pretty little submissive. I'll reward you when you're good, punish you when you break Mommy's—my rules. If you agree, your every pleasure and pain belongs to me...no one else will ever touch you. I'm possessive and controlling, but whatever happens between us will be safe, sane, and consensual. One day when we're ready to outline your rules and our expectations, you'll be given a safeword. All you have to do is say it, and all play ends, sometimes it can get intense and frightening, but all I want is to make you happy."

"We don't have to start tonight?"

I'd already prepared myself to wait. I wasn't surprised by her wanting to put it off until she was more comfortable with giving in to me. We hadn't known each other long enough for the deep level of trust I was going to require of her.

"No, we don't, but one day it will. It's a part of who I am. There's only so much I can compromise on."

"Does that mean we won't, you know, until then?"

I didn't ask permission. I stripped her t-shirt over her head and tossed it to the floor. I cupped the sides of her

45

small breasts, plumped the subtle curves, weighed them in my hands as I circled her dark nipples with the pads of my thumbs.

"Is this what you wanted, baby girl?"

She gave me a jerky nod.

"No, we use our words. You always tell me what you want."

"Yes." Her breaths quickened.

I teased her mouth with mine, tested the plump lines with the edges of my teeth. I moved lower to her breasts, sucking hard at her nipples until she gasped and arched. Her fingers tore at the tie holding my bun in place. The rougher I used her, the more painful the prick of her nails into my scalp. I rolled my tongue around her nipple, learned the texture of it, and the slightly swollen areolas. One then the other, until I ripped her shorts and thong down her legs. I returned my mouth to hers. Just rested my lips on hers.

"You want me to fuck you, little love?"

"Please."

I curved my left hand between her thighs and felt her heat and wetness in my palm. She violently shook as I used my thumb to tease her clit. A feral smirk tilted my lips at the sound of her palms slapping onto the countertop. She lifted and arched her hips.

I circled her tight pussy hole, felt it tighten then give as I slowly slid in my middle and ring fingers. I growled at her clenching around the digits. The harder I finger fucked her, the higher-pitched her moans became. The heel of my hand slammed into her clit, and she forced her legs wider until her thighs trembled. I slipped from her pussy.

"Fuck, baby girl, you gonna come for me?" I tore at the front of my jeans until I had the button undone and the zipper down, I grabbed her wrist and released it as I placed her hand on my neatly trimmed pubes. "Touch me." I twisted her hair around my fist as she slipped beneath the denim. Her touch was hesitant, but I shifted my stance, and I cursed at the first stroke of her fingertips along my slit and my hard clit. Sweat was making my clothes stick to me, and then her touch disappeared.

I took in her expression, and I saw need and panic, her cheeks were flushed, and she was unsure. She'd entered strange territory, and I could tell she was lost. She was so close. I needed her release more than I wanted mine.

"Hold my neck," I ordered, and when she did, I stroked my damp fingers along the cleft of her cheeks and lower until I could thrust back inside.

"I wish I had my strap-on, I'd bend you over and fuck you until you scream for me."

The harder I worked her, the quicker she fucked onto my fingers until her hips were jerking, and our bodies were slamming together. Her breasts were pushed to mine, and she was hugging my neck tightly. I nibbled at the line of her throat exposed to me when her head fell back. She was rutting against my cotton-covered abs, and then she ground against me. A low, agonized moan followed the rhythmic pulsing of her release.

I barely got my shirt off, fighting her embrace and my own need. I shoved one of my hands into my pants and wound her soft curls around my other fingers. I rubbed myself in an almost punishing pace as I roughly took her mouth, tongue fucked her until I came. Then her forehead fell to my shoulder.

I brushed kisses to her cheek, neck, and shoulder. "Baby girl, I'm gonna love playing with you."

"I think you broke me."

I chuckled at the way her thighs quivered, and she

shook with the aftereffects rubbing herself along my forearm where my hand was still tucked inside my pants. She was drawing out every second of her pleasure. I wanted more. Greedily, I wanted to demand she spread out on the island so I could lick her or better yet, fuck her with my strap-on until she begged me to stop. A quickie didn't come close to what I wanted to do to her now that I had her naked in my home. Exposed, with my true needs out in the open.

"Hold on tight, the Mommy Domme in me wants to give you a nice bath and tuck you into bed."

"Yes, please."

I hugged her to me and lifted her off the counter, and then carried her upstairs. Her hard nipples were as plump as the rest of her. Everything about her triggered all my buttons. Plans for takeout abandoned. I'd cook my little love something later after I had her clean, and we napped for a bit. Well, maybe after I got a taste of her. Giving her one orgasm wasn't enough for me.

6

KATY

Damn, we'd overslept, Lindy had cooked me a quick breakfast and made sure she fed me every bite. I protested because I knew how she was about her schedules. She'd quieted me with a kiss and a smile, told me my full belly was more important than a timetable. After we'd gone upstairs the previous night, I'd been too tired for the bath she'd wanted to give me. Instead, we'd showered, and I felt ashamed that I'd momentarily compared my body to hers.

She was tall and slender, but I'd noticed she had silvery lines across her hipbones and dimples in her thighs, faint ones but still cellulite. And I realized no one was perfect. Some would probably hold her up as an ideal from her slender frame to her perfect breasts, but she made me feel sexy and irresistible. Before her, I felt cute and chunky, neither of which bothered me. I found I was more comfortable in my skin since I turned thirty.

I'd never gotten off so hard in my life where I couldn't control my body. The intensity of that brief encounter had frightened me a bit. Even after the orgasm, I'd wanted more.

Her touch in the shower, while it wasn't sexual, it was the most intimate and sensual act I had ever experienced. And it had everything to do with it being her.

I shifted on the passenger seat and glanced at her to catch her smile. She extended her arm and placed her hand on my thigh, her fingers slipping between them. When she flexed her fingers, the corks popped, and I wished I'd worn my heavily padded bra.

"You okay, need to stop?"

"No, I'm fine. I'd just like to get there."

"We don't have much longer. We haven't had a lot of time to talk since last night. Overwhelmed?"

I paused to think about her question. She meant if I was okay with what happened in her kitchen. Yet it was also about the conversation that happened before the sex. We'd gone on our first date six weeks ago, under two months since I'd shown up on her doorstep. I was attracted to everything about her, even her crazy hours at work. She was driven and understood what she wanted, and she stuck to her goals even if they seemed overwhelming. Of course, there were a few canceled dates, but she always showed up the next day for lunch to make sure she spent time with me.

Out of all my previous experiences, she put in the effort and work, and every little thing she did was to make me feel special. No one had ever done that. I was still unsure if this would be long-term. I didn't believe a month was enough time to figure out if you'd get your happily ever after. While I hoped, I was still cautious.

"No, not overwhelmed. Can I ask you something, though?"

"You can ask me anything, baby girl."

"Why the Domme stuff?"

"That might be difficult to answer. I was always dominant. Some people considered me unfeminine because I didn't conform to the edicts of gender stereotyping. I had a few brief relationships back in my early twenties. There was something about taking care of the woman I was with. To make sure she was comfortable. That she always had what she needed. I set a lot of rules before I even knew what I was doing. The first time I gave a non-sexual, correction spanking, it felt"—she let out a heavy sigh—"odd, but strangely right. My girlfriend at the time wasn't as happy about the situation. It was fine for the bedroom, but it stopped at the door. We didn't last, and then I started researching, trying to find out what was going on with me. I stumbled across Domestic Discipline, the dominant or top, takes care of all decisions. Makes sure their submissive is safe and cared for. The dynamic has to be mutually beneficial."

"How?" I understood she wanted me to be ready. She'd started to prepare me last night with the talk, but I'd always saw myself as independent. I didn't require someone to take care of me. I preferred to do all that myself. I paid my bills, worked, and even when I thought about getting married one day, I hadn't seen myself submitting to someone. What she explained fascinated me, but it also made me wary about whether I could make her happy in the long-run or not. I was sure I wanted to see where this would go; I just didn't know if I could give the level of trust she needed.

"Well, it has to be consensual, has to fill a need for the submissive or little, and the dominant. It's a power exchange, but psychologically and emotionally, it must meet the wishes of both parties. Now, for example, you and I, outside our home, no one would know what we do inside unless we share that part. Inside when it's just us, you'd defer to me. I'd take care of all your physical and emotional requirements. We'd set rules and boundaries. Figure out what our hard limits are. You'd be corrected for infractions and rewarded for good behavior."

"What about the Mommy Domme part?" I'd thought about doing an internet search while she drove, but I wanted to know what it meant to her. From my limited knowledge, I assumed every relationship or dynamic were different. Not everyone's needs were the same.

"You'll allow me to care for you. We'd have bath and playtime. You'll let Mommy cuddle you. It's a regression. You'll allow me to nurture your little side and in doing so, allowing me the freedom to take on responsibility of all your care. Our relationship would be based on complete trust in each other."

"Aren't there clubs or something where you can do all that? Maybe take care of that elsewhere?" As soon as the question was out, I realized I didn't want to know. Did she have little girls all over the place? Was I just one of the ones she called little love? I wanted that all for myself. To be the one and only she did all that with.

"Yes, and I've been to quite a few, and for some that works...spending a few hours or an evening just playing out a scene. While I found it mildly satisfying, I require more. I want commitment, just one sub/little that's all mine, and no one else's to play with. Twenty-four-seven, but I don't want to take your independence or spirit. I adore everything about you, Katy. I'm drawn to every facet of your person-ality and when, not if this happens, I want all of you, the little that wants to submit to me and the free-spirited woman who showed up on my doorstep."

"Would we be monogamous? No other littles besides me or girlfriends?"

"I'd belong to you as much as you would to me. I know

people who have an open relationship, where someone has a little that they take care of and a partner. I'm too possessive, and I wouldn't feel comfortable making you have to share me when I couldn't let someone else touch you."

"Good, I don't think I'd be much of a sharer."

"I'll compromise for a while, but at some point, I won't make us live in a relationship that, in the end, will make us bitter and miserable."

"I know, and I'm curious."

As we talked, I studied her profile as she focused on the road ahead. In my heart, I knew she'd never push me to give in. She spoke too much about trust. She was too open. She'd kept the dominant thing to herself, but I understood, if she'd brought this up on our first or second date, I truly believe I would've run scared.

"You know you already let me do some of those things. The first night, when I washed your face and you didn't protest, I knew I was going to get you to have dinner with me. When I invited you over that first night, and you let me feed you. Taking care of you is the easiest thing I've ever done. I won't say my impatience won't get the better of me until you're ready, but I in no way would ever hurt you. Why don't we make our first rule and agreement?"

"Okay, what would it be?"

"Rule one...you and I are mutually exclusive and will discuss all aspects of our relationship with complete honesty. If at any time either of us feels the need to move on, then we will have an open and honest discussion. Could you agree?"

"Agreed, but you're gonna make rules I'm going to break, aren't you?"

"That's up to you whether you break them or not, you'll just have to accept the consequences of doing so."

She rubbed my thigh before putting her hands on the steering wheel, then turning on the signal to take the next exit. I felt more comfortable now that I had her explanation. There were still questions that would come up—a list of rules to follow. A part of my brain whispered that it was what we needed. To give yourself over in submission to someone else demanded trust, but something said it was also freedom. The means to relieve yourself of the burden of stress—responsibility. To be little again and do nothing but get cuddles and baths. I wasn't sure about the correction stuff. No one had even spanked me during sex before. My past partners were a bit on the vanilla side, mostly missionary, maybe a little doggie style, but none of them had curled my toes or made me crave them. With just a kiss, my addiction to her started, and after she'd worked me to an orgasm in the kitchen, I was curious about more.

"What do you say that after this weekend and we learn more about each other, that we plan an evening where you allow yourself to be my little? I'll set everything up. All you have to do is come to my place. You'll learn what I want from you as your Mommy during an age play scene. Then another night, we'll play out a scene with me as your Domme. We'll settle on a safeword, and if the experience isn't for you, we'll stop and work on your comfort level."

"Fair enough. Maybe I'd understand better if I could experience it. I can't guarantee anything, though."

"Then that's what we'll do. I know putting your trust and faith in someone is hard and daunting, but I just want the chance to have you experience it before either of us gets hurt. And also, this takes a lot of communication and talking. This isn't something that happens instantly. It's like any other relationship where respect, trust, and love need to be earned and developed over time."

"I can live with that."

"Good girl. I'm going to stop for gas and some caffeine, do you want anything?"

"Iced tea and a candy bar."

She nodded as she pulled up to the gas pumps. She asked did I want to come in, but I shook my head. I told her I was going to take a walk to stretch my legs. We'd only been on the road a few hours, but I wasn't used to sitting for so long as one time. Living in the city, everything was walking distance away or public transport.

I wanted this weekend of just us. Learning more about each other while spending twenty-four hours a day together. Dating and hanging out were all well and good, but did you ever know someone until you picked up on their odd quirks or habits? I was shocked that for the first time in my life, I wanted it all. We'd agreed to be exclusive. She was going to show a part of her to me to make sure I was comfortable. Maybe it wouldn't work, or I might not like her in the complete dominant role, but I needed to try.

This wasn't just fascination. I felt I could fall for her. I didn't care that she was a woman, and I was suddenly having to label myself differently. Why did it have to mean anything more than at thirty-two, I found the person I could've been waiting for, and it just happened to be a woman? Yes, I was going to have to introduce her to my parents at some point, but by then we'd know if we were on the right track or not.

7

LINDY

I came awake slowly savoring the warmth of my little love curled against my side. She practically passed out after I'd taken her to the beach and boardwalk to play all the games, then go on a few rides. I think it was more a sugar crash than anything. We shared kisses and cuddles, a little make-out session before we'd gone to dinner last night, but other than that, I'd kept it light. I'd given her a lot to think about on the drive there.

It gave me hope that she'd agreed to running a few scenes soon. I wanted to give her a little nudge, not a shove into a lifestyle she wasn't ready for. She was still growing used to the fact she was dating a woman for the first time. Too many quick changes would terrify her. Nice and easy was the way to go—for now.

She slept soundly, and I eased her to her back. She let out the tiniest protest but settled. I rose onto my elbow and looked down at her. With my left hand, I gently combed her curls back from her beautiful face. I drew my fingertips from the hollow at the base of her throat, a figure eight around her nipples, and groaned as she arched. Her skin was like velvet. I paid close attention to the faint lines on her belly. Everything about my baby girl turned me on. I could so easily become obsessed with her, and maybe I already was in some ways.

I assumed I should feel weird about how quickly my feelings had grown. It was new and intoxicating to know I was about to claim her as mine. My gaze followed the path of my fingers, I bypassed her tight, dark curls, and instead stroked her thigh. It didn't take much coaxing to get her to bend her knee and open wide for me. I eased to kneel beside her. I used my middle and index finger to spread her plump pussy lips.

When she shuddered, I paused until she calmed. She was already wet and ready for me. I positioned her leg between mine to hold her open. My pussy clenched as I brushed against her inner thigh. I gathered her response on my fingers and slowly massaged around her tight bottom, tested the resistance. One day I'd fuck her like that, but not until I got plugs to get her ready. I just wanted to test if she liked being played in that way. From the roll and shake of her hips, she'd take me beautifully when it was time.

I shifted until I knelt between her splayed thighs. Still holding her slit open, I took in the dark pink of her wet lips, and the flex of her pussy hole. I wanted to eat her so bad my mouth watered for a taste, but instead, I fucked into her with the tips of my middle and index fingers. Her clit was left untouched. I'd give her that when I was ready. The way her hole gripped and held to my digits as I fucked her with them was sexy as fuck.

Suddenly, I wished I'd brought the new toys I'd gotten for her. One day I'd own every hole, have her filled and held on the edge, denying her until she cried in desperation for the single touch she needed. I brought my right hand up to cup her breast and leaned down. I wrapped my lips around her nipple. A shudder worked through her body. Her fingers went to my hair.

"Hands above your head, baby girl. Keep them there until I say otherwise."

I sunk my teeth into her nipple as I lifted my gaze to find her staring at me through heavy-lidded eyes. I tugged hard until her hands flattened to the headboard.

"Good girl."

"Please." She lifted her hips, trying to rub against my stomach. I straightened until I stared down at her. The flat of my hand connected with her inner thigh.

"No, little love, you're gonna work for it. Show me how much you want to come all over my fingers."

I tortured her breasts until her nipples were dark and swollen from the abuse of my fingers. She fucked herself onto my other fingers. Sweat dampened her face and beaded on her skin. I could get off just watching her work for her release. Every time she tried to sneak clitoral stimulation, she earned another smack to her thigh. Each one made her tighten, and my hand was soaked.

The print of my hand stood out starkly on her pale skin.

"Come on, you can do it."

"I need—"

"I know what you need, and I'll give it to you when I feel you deserve it." My voice lowered in pitch. Dangerous and gruff. She started to move frantically, and I squeezed her breasts, one then the other, until she was grunting and whimpering. Her feet flat on the mattress, her hips held high as she rolled her sexy body.

Teary, panicked eyes locked onto mine, I could see the pleas for me to end the torture. My inner thighs were slick, my clit ached, and my pussy clenched almost painfully at my own need to get off.

"Tell me what you want, baby girl," I ordered as I brought my free hand to place it under her bottom and held her high, my breath teased her clit, and her dark curls were wet from trying to earn her release. "You want your Domme to suck that needy, little clit?"

"Yes, please, anything, I'll give you—" She fought to push each word through the harshness of her breathing, and then I showed her mercy.

I latched onto her clit and suckled on and off, pinched it between my lips until her screams were muffled by her thighs squeezing my head. It was one release flowing into another, and I heard her panic—savored it. I growled as I jerked my fingers from her and shoved my hand between my legs and worked my nub until I was growling around hers. She was jerking and grinding. Her slick pubes teased my nose, and I watched her face as I found my release. Her cheeks were red and flushed. She was playing with her pretty little tits. She collapsed, her bottom coming to rest on my thighs.

She was so exhausted she laid there with her legs opened wide. I didn't hesitate to cover her body with mine. I captured her lips, shared the taste of her release, and held her tight until we both calmed. Her soft hands stroked over my sweaty back.

I smirked at her little hum as she rubbed her breasts to mine.

"You really have to stop doing that."

"Stop doing what, little love?" I bumped her nose with mine as I softly brushed our lips together. I felt her lazy smile.

"Is it always that intense?"

"I hope so. Just wait until I have you at my mercy for playtime."

She whimpered, and I rested my weight on her, my forearms braced on either side of her head as I stroked her hair back from her face.

"I don't think I'll survive."

"Someone hasn't treated my little love right. I have to make up for it. Show you all the ways your Domme and Mommy can take care of you."

"Can we stay in bed all day?"

I traced the trembling lines of her full lips as she spoke and loved the way they turned up at the corners as she smiled up at me. "Check out is shortly, but if you want to stay, I can make that happen. We'll just need to leave very early in the morning."

"You'd do that?"

"Oh, baby girl, you're gonna learn there isn't much I wouldn't do for you."

I saw her shock in the widening of her eyes. The pupils dilated pushing out the pale blue—the navy circle stood out even more beautifully. She was so perfect. My heart broke as I saw the tears slip from the corners, trickle into the hair at her temples. She tried to hold back a tiny sob, but it tumbled free before she could catch it. I soothed and praised until she calmed. I rolled my hips until we came together, her second release brought on a gentle gasp as wetness coated my lower belly.

When her eyes slowly closed once, then twice as she fought to stay awake, I whispered for her to sleep. Once I felt her completely relaxed, and her breathing evened out, I slipped from the bed. I covered her with the sheet and blankets to keep her from getting chilled as I called to extend our stay another night. If she wanted to spend the entire day in bed with me cuddling, then that's what she'd get.

After a quick shower, I left a note on the pillow to tell her I went out to grab breakfast, and I'd be back, but to stay in bed until I did. I'd bathe her when I returned. So many plans and none of them had anything to do with my job or routine. I relished her being my sole focus and realized how much more intense it would get once I taught her how to play.

8

KATY

I was exhausted, but I couldn't stop smiling. If I didn't watch myself, I'd be bouncing in excitement, but I tried to play it cool since I arrived at work thirty minutes late. I was just glad it was a morning shift, and my boss knew it was a rare occurrence that I even took a day off. She just told me to be careful and get there when I could. Cecile had opened, and I caught every look she darted my way.

The weekend was just what I'd needed. No responsibilities. Lindy had taken care of everything. We'd spent hours in bed doing nothing more than talking. Not that I was complaining in any way about the sex part. It was intense, yet comfortable and safe.

The absolute peace I'd felt after she'd awakened me. Through the heat and shock, I knew I was all she was focused on. My pleasure and nothing else. I don't know what happened to me or why the tears had started when she confessed that I'd learn there was nothing she wouldn't do for me. Would that change as we were together longer?

Even as I rolled the question around in my mind, I knew it wouldn't.

I'd asked more questions about our play. When would we go through the scenes she suggested? As apprehensive as I was at first, I was getting excited to see her in different roles. I knew I'd experienced part of it over our time away, but I felt it would be more in-depth. We'd immerse ourselves in the roles. All she'd tell me was she'd give me warning enough to prepare but nothing else.

I wouldn't see her later. She'd told me that there were a few things she needed to take care of and would be in the office until at least ten PM. I wasn't happy about it. Cuddled up to her quickly became my favorite way to sleep.

I realized I was daydreaming too much and was glad that my job was something I could do on autopilot. Cecile and my replacements came from the back. They waited until we switched cash drawers, and then they took over.

"Are you going to tell me what has you so distracted today? I thought having a girlfriend would make you less... whatever this is. Also, you're never late to work."

"Lindy took me away for the weekend, and I wanted to stay an extra night, we misjudged the travel time. That's all."

"Where did she take you?"

I hesitated as I filled out the form as I counted my drawer. I hated this task. It was only done once at the end of a shift, so I normally avoided this chore if I opened. Cecile always took over for me. A few college girls handled the evenings.

"To the beach, registered for an oceanside room, and I didn't have to do anything but let her take care of everything. She picked me up Friday night, I stayed at her place, and we left early the next morning to drive up."

She gasped and started her happy dance. "Spending the night together now? That's new, and you're holding out."

I knew if I mentioned a weekend away what would happen. She wasn't getting details of what we did together. Neither of us were the type to share what happened in our bedrooms with each other. I always got the highlights, the first *I love yous*, and the first overnight, and I knew her and her boyfriend were discussing the living together thing. There were some things, friend or not, that I didn't need to know about a person.

"It's not a big deal."

"It is. Sex in a relationship is a big deal, especially when the people waited for over a month to get busy."

"Who said we had sex? A weekend away doesn't say I owe her orgasms. Her job is demanding. Night dates aren't always easy for her."

"True. How are you handling her job and the imminent coming out?"

I secured the slip of the drawer count in the twenties slot and placed it in the safe for the boss to do the deposit in the morning. I walked out of the room with her on my heels to go to the small breakroom where we stowed our stuff.

"Her work is frustrating, but I knew when I met her that she doesn't work a nine-to-five. She went out of her way to get us an uninterrupted weekend together. I know she feels bad she can't do more. I'm still thinking about the coming out as bisexual thing. When we're together outside I don't hide that we're dating. It feels natural. I'm just worried about how my parents are going to take it. They've always assumed I'd meet a man, get married, and maybe gift them with grandkids."

"Even if you were dating a man, kids aren't a guarantee."

"I know that. And I'm nowhere near ready for that

phase or if ever. Being a mom hasn't been on my list of things to do. It's been less than two months, I'm sure this is serious, and I want it to be. I'm going home for Thanksgiving. If Lindy is comfortable, we'll see if she wants to go with me."

"Meeting the parents, that's a good sign. What about hers?"

"Her parents are overseas. I don't know if she's told them about me yet. Like I said, we're still new, and I'm not sure I'm ready to be caught on camera for the society page."

"That has to be weird."

"It is, but she promised she'd protect my privacy as long as she could. I trust her to keep her word."

"Do you have plans with the girlfriend tonight or want to have a girls' night at my place? Jonnie is working overtime on a construction project that another crew got behind on. Seems the other guys have been slacking lately, and he's having to fix it for his boss."

"Can do. Do I need to bring anything?"

"Maybe some snacks. My freezer is loaded with ice cream, and there's a list of movies I want to watch. For a big, bad construction worker, my man can't handle horror."

"You had me at ice cream but sweetened the deal with horror." The thought of horror movies brought up the ink that covered Lindy's chest and arms. I was surprised to find she didn't have any more. She'd told me she wanted them but didn't have the time to do it. I know the ones she had were easily concealed by her suits.

"Be at my place at six. We'll order pizza, and if you want to crash for the night, bring clothes for tomorrow."

"Thanks. I wasn't looking forward to going home and wondering what Lindy was doing."

"Ah, I remember the beauty of the honeymoon phase,

and then it's just a Neanderthal burping and watching sports on your couch. Foreplay consisting of grabbing his junk and saying, how about it."

"Um, I'm overwhelmed by the romance of it all." I snorted as she rolled her eyes.

"I thought the honeymoon phase would at least last until he moved in. Maybe I should date women," Cecile paused. "Maybe not, my PMS could justify murder. Periods sync, and it'll be a blood bath, in more ways than one."

"On that note, I'm out. I'll be over after I change and pack a bag, see if I can have a few minutes to talk with Lindy."

"I'll see you then."

I left with a wave and decided I needed the walk home and do a bit more thinking. Why hadn't I called my parents yet? I never hesitated before to let them know I was dating a man. It shouldn't be different with Lindy. I slipped my phone from my pocket and hit the speed dial for Lindy. I'd ask her first if it was okay. There was still three months before Thanksgiving.

"Hello, baby girl. Get in trouble for being late?"

"No, it was fine. It's not a habit of mine, and I rarely call off sick. I wanted to ask you something important."

"Anything, you know that."

"I was thinking about telling my parents about us, and if you were okay with it, maybe go with me for the holidays."

"Do whatever makes you comfortable, little love. How do you feel about telling them?"

"Well, I wouldn't hesitate if you were a guy. It seems unfair that I keep it secret."

I wanted to scream it from the rooftops, I was safe and happy, and the physical connection couldn't be hotter. She was attentive and loving, and her devotion to me wasn't to have sex with me—no means to an end.

"I'm okay with whatever decision you make. This isn't something that can be taken lightly. If you feel safe and comfortable enough with me to tell them, then I'll be there no matter the outcome. My home is always your home for a weekend, a night, or the holidays. We'll just make our own traditions."

"I'm sure it'll be fine. They're not judgmental people." I hope I sounded more confident than I felt. My parents never said a bad word about anyone, but I felt it could be different with it being their daughter and not someone else's.

"Then I'll support you. And I'll make sure to threaten my clients to get the holidays off from now on so I can spend them with just you, or your friends and family."

"Thank you." She gave me what I needed so easily, and I had to admit in such a short time that I was spoiled by that.

"Little love, you don't have to thank me for that. That's how a relationship works. We share the good and the bad. Also, I'm not at all happy that I won't be coming home to you curled up in my bed tonight."

"I was thinking the same thing earlier."

"Soon, I promise. What I *do require* is a lot of trust to be placed in my abilities. That means dealing with someone else doesn't always sit well with my clients. If I could change that I would. You should have my sole focus especially this early in our relationship."

"I get it. You weren't secretive that your job was demanding. You didn't think I could do better when you found out about my degree. I miss you, but I'm not the clingy type. If late nights and phone calls, or even just lunch dates are all we get most of the time, I'm okay."

I was surprised it was the truth. I should feel more abandoned, but she'd always made sure when we were together that no one was more important. Maybe down the road it would be a bit too much. Yet it was early stages. We had plenty of time to work out what worked for us.

"I couldn't have asked for a better little love."

"I better be your only one."

"No one else, that title and position are all yours. As of right now, Wednesday evening is completely free, what about you, if you're comfortable, bring an overnight bag? If you don't want to stay, we can just have a quiet dinner, and I'll make sure you get home safely."

"Wednesday it is. I'm going to Cecile's tonight. Her boyfriend is working overtime. We're going to have a girls' night."

"Good, I'm glad you won't be alone. I'll call you at bedtime to tell you goodnight."

"I'd like that."

"Are you ready to have playtime with me?" Her voice dipped low. It was the same when she ordered me to work for my release. And my stomach danced with nerves.

"Yes, but I'm nervous."

"We're going to go at your pace. If you don't like it, all you have to do is say so. Trust doesn't happen overnight. Remember what we talked about."

"I am."

"Good. I have to go, but tonight I'll call, and every night, to make sure my baby girl is being good and getting ready for bed."

I bit my lip and tried not to let my voice crack as I said bye. I disconnected the call and returned my phone to my pocket. How did she have so much power over me already? It should frighten me, but there was an odd flaring of freedom to it. To know that in a few days, all I was going to have to do was let go and trust her. She wouldn't force anything on me. She wanted to make sure I experienced it before we jumped into something I wasn't ready for, and I adored her sensitivity. Trust and care were of massive importance to her. I knew she'd never let me down. All I had to do was make it to our playdate without losing my mind.

9

LINDY

A company based on family values wasn't really the place for their Chief Operating Officer to announce his high-profile divorce and keep his stocks from plummeting. I'll I needed to do was find a way to spin it so that he and his soon-to-be-ex trophy wife were both happy and looked good for the reporters. For twenty years, they played out the perfect couple for the media. Perfect kids, home, and life, arm in arm at the most high-profile events in Ivy Harbor.

Somedays, I hated my job because I fixed other people's stupid mistakes to the detriment of my schedule. It was hard to make friends among your colleagues when you knew some of them covered up the worse of the worst. I tried to keep my morals as in check as possible. Public relations was hell on a person's optimism. I was selective about who I took on.

I unconsciously picked up my phone before I realized what I was doing. My compulsion to contact my baby girl grew, and the weekend hadn't helped my possessiveness. I'd found success and freedom in starting my own firm, answering to no one. Now all of that seemed like a trap. It kept me from the one thing I'd pretended for so long I didn't need. The concept of Katy formed on the night of my birthday until she was a living breathing representation of what I'd promised myself I'd start looking for.

Tossing my phone aside, I picked up the receiver and dialed my parents' number. It didn't matter the time of day, my mother always answered. It was no different, and she didn't bother with a greeting.

"Lindy, what's wrong?"

"Nothing, Mom, I was...I need to tell you something and ask your advice."

"Anything, just give me a moment until I can make it downstairs and put on the kettle. How's work? You're calling from your office."

"Same as always. Husband couldn't keep it in his pants and wanted to exchange the old trophy wife for a younger one."

"The irresistible allure of a beautiful, unadulterated piece of art. We're very much a culture based on the superficiality of beauty standards."

"Are we going to get into the debate of the relationship between symmetrical beauty and the biological imperative to mate? Isn't it a bit late in the night to tear open those old societal wounds?"

She chuckled in that free way she had. Linda Rubin was, for all intents and purposes, the epitome of laidback intellectual. Her place of peace was in the middle of a debate—an exchange of ideas whether they were shared or differing from her companions.

My life had been odd. Always the new kid. And while

people heard boarding school or private school, I didn't grow up with a sense of entitlement. Mom and Dad always said to learn from the mistake of others around you; emulation was the product of mediocrity. They believed that if you didn't stand out, take up space, that you were wasting your potential. Individuality was encouraged throughout my childhood and teen years.

"I can't wait for you to come home. I enjoy your snark much more when I can see your expression."

"Only another year unless Dad decides to find a new university. Someplace more tropical than London."

"I can hope, but I would love to be back in my own home again."

They owned the brownstone beside mine. I didn't hover over the person they hired. She'd worked for my parents for the past decade, either staying or coming by every other day to water the plants or keep the dust down.

"I'm keeping a close eye on it, and your house sitter is keeping your plants alive."

"Now that I have a lovely cup of tea, what's on your mind?"

"I met someone."

I rolled my eyes at her exaggerated gasp as if my meeting someone would throw the world off its axis and send the Earth tumbling into the ether.

"What? When and how? Not someone you work with, please, no."

"No, her name's Katy. She was on a date, and he stood her up, in a moment of deep emotion, she thought she was going to his home. Once she stopped cussing him and realized he wasn't standing in the doorway, I knew she was going to be mine."

"You sound like your dad after he met me. What is she like?"

I sighed and leaned back in my chair. "Perfect." Everything about her was just right. "Smart, sweet, snarky, so beautiful."

"How's she handling your job?"

That was always one of the first questions she asked whenever I told her I met someone. I'd just never gotten this close to introducing someone to them before. To be honest, I was looking forward to sharing her with my family and introducing her to my friends. Planning to make sure she had a place with me. I'd start to bring in more people to take over my workload. Leaving me more time for her.

"Understandably frustrated. It hasn't even been a few months yet. I rearranged things so we'd have the full weekend. We came back early this morning."

"You taking time is a big deal for you, Lindy. I know you're not happy with your life. You've used your job as an excuse not to form an emotional attachment. You may think you're good at keeping secrets, sweetie, but you've lived with us and beside us your entire life."

"Mom, before you continue, my sex life or what that entails, is not up for discussion."

"Of course it's not, I don't want to know what my daughter does with her lovers. We're close but not that close."

"Just wanted to make sure that was clear." She snorted, and I rolled my eyes at her amusement. If there was one thing my mother was good at, it was pushing buttons. My ability to read people came from her. I swore if she'd gone into a life of crime, she'd be the best con artist in history.

"You may be good at spinning tales for your clients, but you're not so smooth when it comes to your life."

"You're going to hurt my feeling, Mother."

"If that was possible, we would have destroyed your psyche years ago."

"I do love these midnight moments of maternal discourse."

"You're always the one who loves calling me in the middle of the night."

"Mom, I just want to make sure...I guess I want...I'm the first woman she's dated. That's a lot of pressure on both of us. Being with me would mean coming out, and history shows that doesn't always end happily."

"Honey, this is the first time you've wanted to make space for another person in your life. Momentous occasion. And I heartily approve of this development. Who we love has nothing to do with our gender. If I'd fallen in love with a woman back in school, I would've taken whatever opportunity to be with that person. She better be around at Christmas when we come to visit."

"Wait, we didn't have plans for Christmas."

"Um, honey, that was before I found out about the girlfriend."

"Shit."

Her cackling wasn't making me look forward to this visit.

"Chin up, honey, you knew what was going to happen as soon as you mentioned her."

"I was cautiously optimistic that the lure of warm ocean breezes and umbrella drinks would keep you away."

"Silly. The lure of my confirmed bachelorette of a daughter finding the woman meant to be hers. I will make sure to swim to Ivy Harbor if I need to. All I know is after thirty-nine years, you're not going to change habits overnight. It's a process. You're making time. You're about to try to cut down your workload, right?"

"Planning on it, but bringing in a team, hiring the right people takes time. I don't want my little love to get tired of waiting around."

"Make the effort. That will go a long way in proving you want her in your life. Just keep doing what you're doing. You're charming, successful, attentive, and if I say so myself, quite beautiful."

"Thank you, okay, I'm going to call her to say goodnight. She's spending the night with her friend since I was working late."

"Go, I'm going back to bed for a few hours until your dad heads off to work, then I'm sleeping more until my afternoon lecture."

"Tell Dad I love him. I love you too. I'll make sure to keep Katy around so you can spoil her when you come for Christmas."

"Do that. I've waited long enough for a prospective daughter-in-law without putting pressure on you. Prepare yourself for the pressure. I want this, Lindy, don't disappoint me."

I pulled the phone away from my ear and realized she'd hung up on me. Full-on *Godfather* voice and all, I didn't take threats from my mother lightly. She may look respectable, but I didn't put extreme psychological torture out of her arsenal of weapons she'd cultivated over her lifetime. I replaced the receiver and picked up my phone from where I left it. Spinning my chair, I stood up to look out over the city, took in the lights glittering on the harbor, and connected a call to my baby girl.

"Hi. I was wondering if you were going to call."

"I said I would, little love. I never break my word to you."

"Are you still at work?" I heard the concern in her question. She didn't comment about my hours, but I also quickly realized that she worried about all the time I spent at work.

"Yes, I just got off the phone with my mom. I told her about you, and she said I better keep you happy. She threatened me if I disappointed her and she didn't get to meet you. I fear for my life, baby girl."

"We can't have that. You're going home soon, right?"

"Shortly. A few more emails. Did you have fun tonight?"

"Too much ice cream and pizza, too much gore."

"As long as you had fun. I want you to get some sleep. You were up early, and you have to open in the morning."

"I will. Lindy?"

"Yes?"

"I wanted to say thank you again for the weekend. I know taking time off isn't easy for you. I don't expect you to change your whole life for me."

"Baby girl, I've told you, I want this to work, and in order for that to happen, I need to start taking steps to make sure we have time together."

"I don't want to pressure you, though. I don't want to be that nagging girlfriend that complains about her person's hours. You always make time when you can. Miss a dinner and have lunch, bedtime phone calls every night we're apart. I don't want you to lose your patience with me."

"It's not pressure. It's demanding the time you deserve from the person you're dating. Wednesday night it's just us, no phones or distractions."

"I look forward to it. Goodnight, Lindy."

"Night, little love, make sure you're a good girl and get your rest."

We spoke a few more minutes then I reluctantly let her go. I went through the last tasks I needed to do before going home. I made plans for Wednesday. I'd have to do a bit of shopping on my lunch break for dinner and something special for my baby girl. Our date couldn't get here fast enough.

10

KATY

I held my overnight bag in a white-knuckled grip and nervously nibbled my bottom lip as I stared at Lindy's door. Since I'd left work, my anticipation turned to fear of the unknown. She'd never hurt me. It was too much too soon. Yet wasn't. I trusted her.

I froze as the door opened slowly, and my breath stilled in my lungs at the suit-clad woman staring at me with something that couldn't be anything other than adoration in her eyes. She didn't say a word or try to touch me, just extended her arm and turned her hand palm side up. Trust. I felt she'd stand there as long as it took for me to decide. I could walk inside, share dinner, watch TV, and spend our night like any other. No scenes. No playtime.

My fingers ached as I release the firm, leather handle of my bag. I placed my hand in hers, and she gently pulled me inside.

"Hello, little love." She leaned down to kiss me, and I didn't hesitate to tip my chin up to meet her halfway.

"Hi."

"There is no need to be nervous here. This is our home.

Our safe place. What happens inside these walls is between us. Whether I'm your Mommy, Domme, or Lindy, you will always be my number one concern. Your consent means everything to me."

She removed my bag and left it beside the door. "You won't need that tonight. I bought you everything you need."

I swallowed hard around the lump in my throat.

"What happens now?"

"After we have dinner, I'm going to take you upstairs. Give you a nice long bath so that you're relaxed. Then I'm going to dress you. All night you're going to trust me just to...take care of you."

"What about rules?"

"I'll tell you all about them while I bathe you."

She led me to the kitchen and seated me at the table. I sat there with my hands folded on my lap, and she leaned down and pressed a kiss to the corner of my mouth.

"All you have to do for me tonight is be my little."

I nodded, and she moved away from me. I tried to calm my breathing as I felt myself panting. She always pampered me when we spent time together, but this was different from that. She asked me to let go. I trusted her. I had no doubts that she'd never intentionally hurt me physically or emotionally. An adult-sized sippy cup with a soft, silicone mouthpiece was set on the placemat in front of me. It looked as if it contained milk.

She didn't linger. She made two plates, and when she returned to the table, she put both in front of her as she sat down. She had a purple one with three sections and a plastic spoon in the same bright shade. My embarrassment made me hesitate as she held out a spoonful of cut-up spaghetti and sauce. I barely kept myself from protesting, and then I did as she asked of me. I trusted her to make sure all my needs were met. She praised me after each bite, wiped my mouth, and told me to take a sip of my drink. It seemed to take three times as long for her to make sure we'd had enough to eat. But not once did she rush me.

It was just the two of us with no time limit on our evening together. When we finished, she had me help dry the dishes. Just small tasks a parent would ask of their little girl.

"Are you ready?"

I nodded, and she took my hands in hers. She was holding them as she backed up and led me upstairs to her room. I didn't know what was happening except for what she outlined. She positioned me on the mat beside the tub, and I watched every move she made. She started with her jacket, removing it slowly, and as if she had all the time in the world, she strode to the doorway where a series of hooks were hung to the right of it. She placed her jacket on one of them, and she returned to me, rolling her sleeves up to her elbows. I followed the ascent as it exposed the ink from mid-forearm up to where it was hidden beneath the linen.

"Little love, do you need to go potty before your bath?"

She crouched down by the tub and started the water. She tested the temperature, running her fingers through the stream until she seemed satisfied. She popped the top on some bubble bath. She called my name, and I realized she'd asked me a question.

"Yes, ma'am."

"Mommy, for tonight, that's all you'll call me."

"Mo...Mommy." She lifted my dress, pushed my panties down, and lowered me onto the toilet seat. She didn't move away. I held it thinking she'd find something else to do.

"Little love, you need to potty before your bath." Her tone was stern, much like the night she'd told me it was unsafe to go to strange men's homes. I realized she'd fallen into her Mommy Domme persona since day one.

I opened my mouth to argue, but the look she gave me had me closing my mouth, and my teeth clicked. My face stung with the intensity of my shame as I forced myself to unclench and pee. My eyes kept moving over the room and focusing on anything but her.

"Good, baby girl."

The praise made it worse, but I kept reminding myself even though it was embarrassing, she'd done nothing but wait for me to obey. Almost as if she was giving me time to process. When I was done, she'd wiped me, and I stood. It was odd. There was nothing sexual in the way she removed my dress, sandals, or even my panties. It was pampering or actions of a—Mommy. She took my hand and helped me into the tub, easing me into water that was just right. I sighed as I sank into the bubbles, and when I caught her gaze, she was smiling down at me.

"Tip your head back. I'm going to wash your hair before I bathe you."

I obeyed as she worked her fingers through my hair, her blunt, perfectly trimmed nails scored my scalp. I didn't remember anyone ever washing my hair. A sigh slipped out, and I relaxed completely into her care. I just allowed myself to trust her, and isn't that what she'd asked of me?

"I know I asked before, but why do you like being a..."

"Caretaker. Mommy. Domme."

"Yes, those?"

"Some of us are born naturally dominant or submissive, but it's not everything that we are. It's just a part of us. Society favors the dominant...the successful. We're looked at as the ones at the top of the food chain. We're revered. For some, they live an act. High-powered businesspeople, cops, people in positions of power going from work to dungeon to feed their submissive side. Because we're forced into roles. Or in my case, people see me one way. Controlled and sometimes cold, but I want to come home to someone I can care for and nurture. This part of me isn't about sex."

"But your Domme..."

I opened my eyes as she stripped the last of the shampoo from my hair and found her smiling down at me.

"You don't have to be shy or unsure about asking questions. Bisexuality and accepting your submissiveness is a huge revelation. It's not something that can be easily understood and packaged, especially with someone like myself."

"I just don't want to drive you away if I can't do all this right off."

"Didn't I say we'd take our time? Trust doesn't happen instantly. Sometimes it takes months for you to find that level. Now, little love, sit up, so Mommy can finish washing you."

She did as she claimed, she bathed me. It was tender, but I couldn't stop my body from reacting as the cloth stroked my breasts, lightly brushing my nipples.

"It's okay, baby girl, our bodies respond to being touched...caressed. Spread your legs for Mommy. I need to make sure you're all nice and clean."

I braced my hands on either side of the tub and spread my thighs apart. It wasn't like when we'd had sex. She tenderly cleaned me.

"Ready for your rules? They'll apply to our time together."

"Yes, Mommy."

I gasped as she pinched my clit between her cloth-covered fingers. It didn't go further than that. My body responded to her touch. I knew the intensity of pleasure I reached with her. She said no sex when I was little with her. But what if I asked her for what I wanted; would she reward me for being her good baby girl?

"Just lie back and listen. I have them written down and printed out. You'll sign the agreement when you're done being little."

My heartbeat quickened as I rested my nape on the rim of the tub and found her watching me.

"This is an individual experience; no two people are alike in what they need. We've already established rule one...we will always be honest with each other and exclusive until we decide that doesn't work for us."

She dragged her slender fingers through the bubbles floating atop the water. I traced her features with my gaze, took in the way she looked at me. It was still amazing to me that her adoration was all for me. I'd dated, nothing serious, but this was completely different from the times before. Even in the early stages, I'd never felt special.

"Now, let's build on those rules. Rule two...you will always put your care in your Mommy's or Dommes' hands. In the rooms of this house or places where we're comfortable, you will allow me to take care of you completely. Only I will meet your needs."

Her intense stare locked with mine, and I agreed.

"Rule three...if you break any of the rules set forth and agreed upon, you will earn punishment at my discretion. That could be a paddling, spanking with a bare hand, or corner time. Fighting me will only make it last longer and possibly more painful. But punishing you will hurt me greatly, as I don't want to cause you pain. That doesn't mean I won't do it if necessary."

Again, I agreed. Each rule was different. A lot of them

non-sexual in nature. I'd anticipated differently from the few romance books I'd read. It was mainly about allowing her to take complete control of my needs. Like the caretaker she'd mentioned before. She wanted to be allowed to nurture me like she wasn't allowed to do in her everyday life. Some of my nervousness eased away with the outlining of the rules. She informed me she could add rules as our relationship grew. She told me my safeword. I was to use it if our times together became too intense or uncomfortable. She made sure I repeated it and that I knew at any time, no matter what we were in the middle of, I had the right to withdraw consent. She'd stop with no questions asked.

When she was done, she slowly straightened and picked up a towel. She told me to let the water out and stand, and I did as she asked. I reached to take the towel from her, and she shook her head.

"No, you're mine, our rules put into place, and that means this is my task. Tonight, you're just here for me to spoil."

"Yes, Mommy."

"Good, little love."

She covered my head and squeezed the water from my curls, being easy not to rub them dry. I didn't want my hair to be a frizzy mess by the time she was done. All my nerve endings rushed to the surface of my skin as she tenderly dried me from head to toe. Her touch wasn't meant to arouse, but my body thought otherwise. I gripped her shoulders as she lifted my right leg to rest my foot on the edge of the tub. I sighed as she slowly moved the cloth between my thighs. She groaned as my nails dug into her.

By the time she finished, a slight trembling took over, and my knees felt weak. I was on autopilot as she fixed my hair into small twists on either side of the crown of my head.

I noticed that not once had she taken her attention from me. She helped me into bright yellow panties and then a sleeveless gown with ruffles around the armholes, collar, and hem that hung to just above my knees.

She got my toothbrush ready for me, and I cleaned my teeth as she straightened up the bathroom.

"What are you thinking, baby girl?"

"I like this."

"I hope you do because I want you to enjoy your time or life with me."

Her easy smile caused my own to tilt at the corners. Her wink made me blush as she told me to finish up. I was shocked to find I was impatient to find out what happened next. Would I get to watch TV, would she read me a story, all these things I remember from when I was little flashed through my head. I rinsed my mouth and brush, and after I was done, she laced her fingers through mine.

I'd only ever seen her bedroom on the third floor, and I realized there were two rooms on the second level that I'd never paid attention to. One door was open and revealed a home office. The other one was closed, and when she pushed it open, there was a single bed with baby-blue comforter and pillows cases. Toys overflowed from a toy chest in the right corner, but what drew my attention the most was the oversized rocking chair. The arms were padded, along with ones on the seat and back.

"What's this?"

"This is the room we'll use when it's Mommy and little girl time. In this room, you can regress as much or as little as you want, but I felt you needed separation. So this is our place."

"You did this for me?"

"Of course, look around."

"You didn't have to do anything special."

"This is new for you. Until you're more comfortable, this is where we'll have our playtime and where you can safely go to be little."

I walked the edge of the room, peeked into the closet to find dresses and gowns, and it was perfect. Everything about it was geared to make sure I was happy. I glanced over my shoulder to find her crossing the room toward the rocking chair. She dragged a blanket from the foot of the bed and then seated herself on the chair.

"Come here. Mommy is going to rock you."

I shyly crossed the room and sat down sideways on her lap. I let her position me how she wanted, my face buried in the curve of her neck, and her left arm was wrapped around me. She cradled me on her lap and against her chest. I felt the smile pull at my mouth as she began to rock. She told me stories, and when I fidgeted, she patted my bottom, then restarted the back and forth motion. All the day's tension of a busy day at work and the five dogs that needed walking, it melted away in the steady rhythm of the chair—the soothing cadence of her voice as she told me tales of Princesses and their female Knights or Queens. All tales of happily-ever-afters, and at that moment, I wouldn't change this for anything in the world.

Maybe I'd never seen myself falling for a woman or finding peace in being her little or sub, but as much as I thought I'd feel awkward, I discovered this felt just right.

11

LINDY

Her shy expression flashed through my memory a hundred times that day. I'd held on tighter for a few minutes as I opened the door of the car that I'd requested for her. She'd slept so beautifully in the cradle of my arms as I'd rocked her to sleep. I knew she'd waited for my touch to turn sexual, but that wasn't what being my little was about. When it was time to fuck her, she'd cry and plead for her release.

Gary had dropped me off at home an hour earlier, and I was preparing for when she'd arrive. My Domme side was impatient to be set free. If she'd thought our other nights were intense, I couldn't wait to see how she reacted to submitting to my complete control.

I'd told her she didn't have to bring anything but herself. When I'd shopped to prepare her room, I'd thrown in a few more items. Clothes for my big girl to wear. I had spread out the red dress on the foot of the bed, with a pair of matching stilettos. All night she'd be bare beneath the dress except for silk stockings and a garter belt.

For me, this was going to be a special night. I opened the

jewelry box and fingered the delicate gold chain that would be snug around the base of her neck. Once she accepted my symbol of possession, then nothing stood in our way. To be honest, I'd never been this nervous before, and I wasn't ashamed to admit that. Collaring my one and only was something I'd always dreamed about.

I couldn't believe only months had passed since I'd met her. It felt like longer, and I wanted everything with her, and this was the final step in showing her she was it for me. I'd drawn up our contract and printed it out, but tonight she wouldn't be my little girl. Our toys were prepared and laid out on the long, narrow table along one wall. All that was left was for me to get dressed.

I'd ordered a special meal; the chef and his server would arrive any minute to set up the dining room for a romantic dinner. I knew nothing was always perfect, but it was as close as I could get. It seemed as if I'd waited a lifetime for my perfect little and sub to stumble into my life. Now that she was there, I wasn't taking any chances I'd ruin that.

My hair was smoothed into a bun, not a single strand out of place. My clothes were hung on the back of the closet door, perfectly tailored and pressed. I was unsure of the next step, but she needed to see that part of me. I picked up the harness from the dresser top and bent to slip my legs into the holes of the straps. As I straightened, I slid it up my leanly muscled legs. Once I had it all the way on, I adjusted the buckles to make sure it was secure. I stroked the thick, five inches of veined Packer.

My chest tightened at the weight of it in my palm and the vision of sinking into my little love after we had dinner and drinks. The uncut, realistic dildo bent with a series of connected beads, and I eased it into a downward angle, then covered it with my boxer briefs. I rubbed the bulge and watched as my tightly furled nipples became harder. I was already imagining all the things I would do with my little love.

I didn't have time to linger, I quickly dressed, and slipped on my black heels. Just as I made it downstairs, the doorbell chimed, and I opened it to find the chef. Roberto was an old friend from college. He'd worked as a short-order cook, and I'd slung booze in the bar. We'd become fast friends, and it had lasted over the years.

"Lindy, is your woman here yet?" he asked as he leaned in, and I offered him my cheek.

I laughed at his flustered question. He'd always had an abundance of energy that he never knew what to do with.

"No, you have an hour before she arrives."

"Perfect. I can't ruin this special night."

"I'm just glad I was able to get you to come here tonight. I know how busy the restaurant gets."

"For you, I'd give up a night off or two. The hard-assed Lindy Rubin is getting engaged-ish."

I motioned him and the server he introduced as Maria inside. I stayed in the kitchen to catch up as he unpacked everything he'd need. Maria went about setting the table, candles, china, and everything else. I would have driven myself crazy trying to get all of that done.

"So, are you ready?"

"I hope so."

"Big step, Lindy. I've noticed you getting more and more discontent over the years. The woman I knew from the old days seems to be back."

"My baby girl is perfect."

He poured me a glass of wine, and I checked the time every five minutes. I didn't know why I was so nervous about making the commitment. My little love was everything I'd always wanted, but I also knew this was foreign territory for her. I worried as time progressed that doubts hidden beneath the pristine surface of the newness would eventually crack and reveal themselves. Part of me was still waiting for that. Also, this wasn't a few nights of scenes to satisfy us both. No, this was permanence. Yet I had to keep reminding myself we hadn't agreed to exclusivity that long ago.

Trust didn't happen overnight.

The sound of the doorbell pulled me from my wandering mind and the sporadic conversation I'd attempted with Roberto. I slipped off the stool and strode to the front of the house and opened the door. My baby girl was beautiful.

"Good evening, little love."

"Hi, you look gorgeous."

"And you're as beautiful as ever. Come in. I have to get you ready for dinner."

I saw insecurity flare as she glanced down at her pretty dress. I shook my head at her and slipped my arm around her to bring her inside.

"Baby girl, there's nothing wrong with what you're wearing, but I got you a few presents, and I want you to wear them for me."

She hugged my waist and let me lead her upstairs to the bedroom. "You don't have to keep buying me things."

"I know I don't have to. I want to." I closed the door behind us and knew we had about thirty minutes to wait for dinner. I released her, and her sharp gasp alerted me she'd spotted the items spread out on the bed.

"It's...I don't even know..."

I tracked her every movement as she stroked the silk with her fingertips. I didn't hesitate to step up behind her, and my packer pressed to her lower back, and she froze. Instead of drawing attention to it, I raised my hands to ease the dress down her arms, until it pooled around her feet.

"Do you know what's going to happen tonight, little love?"

"N—no."

I released the front clasp of her bra and pressed a kiss to her shoulder. "Do you trust me, baby girl?"

"Of course."

I loved how she instantly relaxed against me. The trust was there. I needed to be patient with those three little words I wanted to hear from my baby girl. I slipped around her and finished stripping her, giving her soft brushes to her mouth until I had her naked in front of me.

"You're so beautiful. Just right." I cupped her breasts and pinched her nipples between my fingers. She whimpered and leaned into my touch. "Always so needy."

"Is that bad?"

"You needing me is never bad. I want you to bend over the bed for me."

"Yes, ma'am."

She didn't linger and eagerly bent over, exposing her plump ass. I picked up the bottle of lube, slicked the fingers of my right hand, and then spread her cheeks with the left.

I groaned as she rolled her hips into my touch, and she tensed as the tip of my middle finger breached her tight, back hole.

"Anyone ever fucked your ass before?"

"No, ma'am. It felt odd when you told me to—"

"Told you what?"

"To prepare my bottom for you." I knew when I'd sent her home with the enema kit that she'd been embarrassed by my request. She'd assured me she wanted to do it the first time, and I'd allowed that. I wanted her to be comfortable and knowledgeable about everything we did together.

"This pleases me. I'll own every inch of you."

"Yes, ma'am."

The next item I picked up was the slim plug, just a starter one to get her used to her ass being filled. I wanted to own every piece of my little love. I slicked the plug and slowly fucked her with it, loving the way she met each thrust. I heated her pale ass with several swats until she was shifting her thighs farther apart. I slipped my left hand beneath her and tortured her clit. A panicked moan sounded as the thickest part slipped inside.

"Fuck, you're wet for your Mistress."

I smacked her pussy lips.

"Make me cum, please, Mistress."

I loved the way she stuttered over *Mistress*.

"No, not until we're done with our date. My little love gets pleasure when I feel like it."

She was shaking, and her flushed face appeared as I straightened her. I ordered her to stay, and I went to the bathroom to wash my hands. I brought a warm, wet rag back into the bedroom and cleaned the lube from her bottom, but left her slick between her thick thighs.

I knelt in front of her and dressed her in the garter, stockings, and the heels. I couldn't resist a taste. I kept her heel resting on my thigh as I leaned in. I pushed my tongue between her lush pussy lips. I slowly licked her clit and then deprived her of my presence as I stood. When I finally slipped the dress over her head, I smoothed it over her plump body.

She simply stared at me as I led her to the vanity and bench that I'd bought for her. I lowered her to the seat, and she gasped. I knew the plug had shifted. I prepared her for dinner by doing her hair.

"Do you like your presents, baby girl?"

"I love them. I feel full."

"I know, but I started you off with the smallest one. We'll work you up until you're ready to take your Mistress' cock. Do you want that?"

"Are you going to take me tonight?"

"Only your pussy and mouth. Your mistress doesn't want to hurt you unless you break my rules."

"I know. I trust you."

"Let's go to dinner. I have a Chef friend of mine making us something special."

I caught her shy smile in the mirror. I knew my attentions still overwhelmed her, but I wanted to give her everything she deserved, and in turn, she'd gift me with her trust and hopefully love.

12

KATY

Mommy and Mistress weren't that different. I shifted on her knee where she was feeding me dinner. The chef and server had left once dinner was served, and he said he'd return the next day for the items he left behind. He seemed nice enough, but I wanted time for the two of us. I took the last spoonful of chocolate mousse, and then she wiped my mouth.

I automatically took a sip of wine. As always, being with her was easy. Comfortable silences and relaxed conversation, she touched and kissed me freely. I didn't think I'd ever missed someone as much as I did her when we were apart. Even sitting there with my bottom filled with a plug and no panties, I felt no discomfort at all. The quickness of my arousal as she'd ordered me to bend over the bed shocked me. I'd never thought about anal play with anyone I'd dated, but nothing felt taboo with her. I knew that with a single word, she'd stop no matter what.

"Did you enjoy dinner, little love?"

"It was great. No one has ever had a chef make me a private meal before."

"You deserve to be pampered. I've told you before I love spoiling you. And speaking of spoiling."

I laughed as she reached into her inside jacket pocket, and she removed a slim jewelry box. She opened it, and the hinge creaked slightly. A delicate gold chain rested on black silk.

"This is our promise. You wear this as a symbol that you belong to me. That you gave yourself to me without a doubt that I will always care for you. That your every need will always be my top priority."

My hand shook as I traced the chain with my fingertips —my collar—and I knew what it meant. She'd explained that when she found her one and only, she'd give her a symbol of ownership. She always told me she wanted to keep me, but this was tangible. It was proof that I was hers, and she was mine.

"Will you wear it for me, little love?"

"Yes." I didn't have to debate my answer. This was right, and it had felt that way since the night I'd shown up on her stoop. I held my breath as she removed the chain and gently put it on me. I slowly exhaled as she kissed the cool metal, and as weird as it might be, I'd never felt as if I belonged until the moment I found her and my place in the world. My life had led up to being claimed by her, and one day, I'd tell her how much I cared—how much I loved her. It happened so quickly, I didn't second guess myself, but I needed just a bit more time to process.

She combed her fingers through my hair until they caught in my messy bun and tugged my mouth down to hers. I closed my eyes at first contact. All she had to do was give me one of her looks, and I was wet. Her lips were soft. She didn't force me, and every word or action was an uncon- scious seduction. I parted my lips slightly as she changed angles, her tongue stroked over my bottom lip. I didn't censor or hold back. I was always safe with her. My comfort and safety were always her top priority.

I jerked my gaze to hers when she pulled back and began to move the plates and silverware to the side.

"Stand up and then kneel for me."

I didn't argue as I eased off her thigh and lowered to my knees between her spread legs. My breathing kicked into overdrive as I watched her beautiful hands work her belt loose. I swore I could count each slight pause of the rasping as she unzipped her pants. I'd felt the bulge of her strap-on all night, against my back, stomach, and my hip as she fed me. It excited me that she was going to fuck me.

"Who owns you, baby girl?"

"You do, Mistress." A gasp slipped free as a pale, uncut dildo appeared from the V of her open pants. She stroked several thick inches and my pussy clenched, I whimpered as my ass tensed around the plug.

Her hand fisted in my hair, and she jerked me forward. She teased my lips with the fat head.

"Open for me."

Her voice was nothing more than a gruff whisper. My eyes went to hers, her lids were heavy, and I opened my mouth around the tip. It felt odd on my tongue, firm and slightly warmed by her body.

"Suck it, baby girl. Show me how much you want it."

I fucked my mouth with her thick length, grunting, and saliva ran down my chin when I took too much.

"My girl looks so pretty with her mouth stuffed full of cock."

She was holding the base, and I could tell she was working her clit as I sucked her.

"Relax." It was the only warning I got before she pulled

me forward. I swallowed around the head and gagged. She relented for a minute and repeated until I was shaking, tears streaked down my cheeks, and then she jerked me away. Her mouth slammed down on mine, and she fisted her hand in the front of my dress and pulled. The low neckline easily exposed my breasts. My nipples were so tight they ached, and my thighs were slick almost to my knees from hours of teasing seduction.

"How wet are you? Show me. I want you on the table on your knees with your dress exposing that ass filled with your plug and head down."

I barely got to my feet, and I turned, awkwardly crawled onto the table. When I exposed myself for her and rested my head on my crossed arms, I felt raw but free. I rolled my hips as she touched me with just the tips of her fingers, but I was so ready that her gentle stroke was almost painful.

"You love when your Mistress fucks your mouth."

"Yes, Mistress," I screamed as her palms connected with my exposed bottom. I clawed at the table when, without warning, she latched onto my clit.

"Fuck, that fat little clit is so hard for me."

I threw my head back as two fingers entered me, stretching me, and she hit my G-spot. I fucked myself onto her fingers.

"Naughty girl. You didn't ask for permission to take Mistress's fingers."

She tortured my pussy and spanked my ass. I still rode them and took my punishment. Then all sensation ended, and I collapsed on the table. I squeezed my thighs together trying to get that last bit of pressure I needed to orgasm, but I couldn't.

"Mistress, please." I shamelessly begged and cried as I slipped off the table. I sat on her lap, trapped the thickness between my thighs, and worked the veined length along my clit. I squeaked as I was suddenly pushed over the table. Her hand came to rest between my shoulder blades and held me in place.

I froze as the head of the cock started to stretch my hole, and I canted my hips upward. My stilettos gave me just enough height that it was easy to show her I wanted more.

"So wet and swollen, my baby girl's pussy is begging to get fucked."

Sweat made the silk of my dress stick to my skin, and the cool air chilled my exposed bottom. She fucked me with only a few inches, nowhere near enough. This was punishment for not following the rules. I was caught between the need to push back to feel every inch and fear that if I did, she'd stop. I'd never craved like this.

I gasped as she pulled my hair and forced me to straighten. Her breath teased my ear.

"You're going to go upstairs, strip and lie down in bed. Your legs will be open and your pussy and filled ass on display for me. Understand?"

"Yes, Mistress."

As if I couldn't deny her anything, I made my way up to her bedroom. My thighs shook and how wet I was embarrassed me. I cleared my head and did as she asked. I exposed every inch of my body for her. The rolls of my tummy and my dimpled thighs and ass, she loved them all. I'd always been happy with my body. Yes, it was bigger, and sometimes past partners made me self-conscious, but she never had. She made every extra inch of me feel sexy.

I crawled onto the bed and stretched out on my back. My gaze went to the doorway as she came through it. She set bottles of water on the dresser. Her lips curved into a smirk as I drew my legs to the sides and showed her my pussy and the base of the plug. Submissive yet powerful, that's all I could think, I was acquiescing to her, but I was still in control if I used a single word.

"You remember your safeword, baby girl?"

"Yes, Mistress." I swallowed hard as I followed every movement as she removed her clothes. She didn't stop until she wore only the straps of her harness and the weight of the dildo that bounced with each step. I clenched at the memory of swallowing around it and the sensation of my pussy being filled with only a few inches.

"What are you thinking?"

"What it will feel like when you fill me."

"Soon, baby girl, but first..."

My eyes widened as she picked up lengths of rope from the top of a table I'd never noticed before. Her body moved in a languid pace to me. Long moments passed as she wrapped the rope in intricate patterns up my legs and secured them until my heels almost touched the lower curves of my ass cheeks. The caress of the rope was a seduction in itself. Soon she had my legs from ankle to mid-thigh wrapped, and she tied the ends around the bedposts. My bottom was off the bed, and nothing about me was hidden from her.

She returned to the table to pick a few more items and crawled onto the bed. She lowered her mouth to my clit, teasing it lightly with the tip of her tongue. A barely-there caress and I was secured tightly to the point I couldn't move.

"I love the taste of you. These soft curls teasing my nose."

I moaned as she tongued the rim of my pussy hole. I protested as she straightened but stopped at the expression on her face. No one had ever looked at me like that before. Her hands lightly caressed and massaged my body, then the dildo was riding my slit, and her thighs were tucked under me.

"All I want you to do is feel, baby girl. Feel how much I need you. How much it pleases me to love on you."

I clawed at the pillow when the tip of a vibrator lightly touched my engorged clit, and she was sliding deep.

"Mistress makes you cum, and then you're going to suck me until I get off, but you first."

She deep stroked my pussy until she rocked my body. Her small breasts swayed, and her muscles stood out starkly beneath her lightly tanned skin. I was at her mercy, and she used my body, tortured my clit, and I lost count of how many tiny orgasms I had as I felt a larger one trying to tear me apart.

"Fuck, you should see how dirty my little slut looks. You like when I fuck you in deep strokes, but I'm gonna make you beg before I let you taste my pussy."

Her voice was guttural and broken, she slammed into me in shallow thrusts, and just when I didn't think I could take anymore, she turned up the power on the vibe and pressed it hard to my clit. Her hips slapping against me. The double penetration of the plug and her cock stretched me to the point of discomfort, but it only made me want it more.

The wet sex sounds, our moans, and her growled words filled the room. It sounded dirty and taboo, and I couldn't get enough. My body twisted, fighting at my restraints, and my pussy contracted painfully around her cock. She forced her way into my spasming pussy until I felt the agony of the building release hit me. She slammed all the way in and held still as I shook and screamed her name.

I begged her to stay, but she pulled out. I was too ravaged by my release to be shocked when she straddled my shoulders.

"Suck your cum from my cock, baby girl."

I didn't hesitate to suck my release from the length greedily. The suckling noises were loud, and she was breathing heavily. I watched as her beautiful breasts with their dark tips heaved as she fucked my mouth. Then the firm length of her cock slipped from my mouth, and her soaked pussy came down onto my mouth. I licked and sucked, her dildo resting on my forehead, and I didn't care how I looked; all I wanted was to taste her. She rode my tongue until her smooth movements turned jerky and she gripped my hair, my name huskily spilled from her lips. Her orgasm soaked my face.

Another small release hit me at how powerful I felt that I'd given her pleasure, and then she was between my thighs. I moaned in relief as the pressure on my hips released as my legs fell to the bed. I rubbed against her belly, and we kissed deeply, until they turned soft and lazy. She praised me and stroked my body with the tenderest of caresses. I didn't crash like the first time overwhelmed by her focus on my ecstasy. She eased me from the high, and yet I still felt outside myself. The drunken feeling relaxed me until I was close to dozing off.

"Did I make you feel good, little love?"

"Yes. You always make me feel good."

"And that will never change. You were so good. Fuck, I've never been as happy as the night I met you and our months together. You were meant to be mine." She kissed the chain where it rested at the hollow of my throat.

I didn't realize tears were slipping from my eyes until she was kissing them away, and it was a long time later until she removed the ropes, and Mistress became Mommy as she bathed and dressed me.

13

LINDY

"**F**uck," she screamed as I took her bent over the bed, and her nails clawed at the messy covers. I pulled her cheeks apart so I could see the thick, veined shaft of my dildo splitting her abused pussy wide. I had the butterfly-shaped vibrator right on her clit. Her sexy, plump ass shook as my hips connected with her cheeks. She let out a choked cry and fell to the bed, my length slipping free.

I laid down and rolled to my back.

"Make me come," I ordered, and I lifted the slick dildo to rest on my stomach, and she clawed her way onto the bed. She buried her face between my thighs. She sucked my clit. "My little love"—I grunted as I sunk the fingers of my free hand into her hair—"is a natural at eating her Mistress' cunt."

My stomach sucked in tight as I held her in place and ground against her face until I released hard. Fuck, she always got me off so quickly. It had been three weeks since I'd taken her and taught her how to please her Mistress. She was a slutty little girl. When I told her to give me head, she couldn't get on her knees fast enough. She sprawled between my thighs with her head on my belly and her little hand wrapped around my cock. She sucked her taste from it and let out the dirtiest whimper.

"You love the taste of you on my cock, don't you?"

She hummed an affirmative, then let the length slip from between her lips, and her pink tongue licked the plump curves. The vibrator was still working her clit, and she was humping the bed. I allowed her her fun and then hit the switch to turn it off. Every morning if she was with me or not, I made sure I cleaned out her bottom and stuffed her with a plug. We'd almost gotten to the size that she'd be ready to take my strap-on.

I knew her anticipation built every day that I didn't take her. I knew how much she loved her ass played with. She'd confessed that it embarrassed her, but I'd assured her there was no shame between us. If it brought both of us pleasure, then nothing was wrong with how we got off.

"Sit on your Mistress' cock." I observed her as she removed the vibe and tossed it aside.

She lazily climbed on top of me, and she held the base as she slid easily down the thick length. Her thighs shook, and she moaned greedily as she bottomed out, the plug pushed deeper. I stroked her thighs and hips as she rode me in shallow, tight rolls of her body.

"Mistress' little slut."

"Only yours, Mistress."

I raised my hands to play with her abused nipples. Her breasts bore the print of my hands. I was pleased with her acceptance of pain with her pleasure. Her bottom carried the marks of my hand, paddle, and flogger—her back striped from the strips of leather.

"Mistress?"

"Yes, little love?"

"Would Mommy ever touch me like my Mistress?"

"You want Mommy to love on you? That part of our relationship doesn't have to be sexual."

"I know, but—"

I was patient as I waited for her to finish, yet her face heated, and she tried to look away.

"No, we don't hide from each other. But what, don't be shy, just say it. We always agreed to be honest."

I sensed the moment she relaxed, and she drew lazy circles on my sweaty stomach.

"It's always so intense and—"

I put her out of her misery because she wasn't finding the words she wanted.

"You want to be loved on. Taken slowly."

"Yes. We're still in the honeymoon phase. Everything is new, and I've never gotten off to the point it was painful before. You're always so focused on making sure I always experience it without shame."

"If you ever want to just have Lindy and Katy time, no Mistress or Mommy, just us, all you have to do is say so."

"No, it's always just us. I love the care, our rocking chair, and baths. You dressing me in my baby girl gowns and reading me my stories." She huffed. "I'm not doing this right." She tried to get up, and I gripped her hips to hold her in place.

"You love our relationship, the dynamic we have, and I want to keep it the way it is. I want to keep you for a long time, little love. Your happiness is everything to me. If you need something more, then we'll discuss it. We already know you're not a baby, your little is toddler age. Your submissive loves to be fucked with just the right amount of pain. I know every spot on your body that makes you gasp or moan, how you tip your hips to signal you want to be fucked deeper and harder. There will never be shame between us."

"I love being your little girl and your submissive. I guess I was wondering if we'd change at some point."

"Every dynamic changes over time. It's ever-evolving. Maybe you want to regress younger at some point. Maybe you want to be Mommy's naughty brat. Whatever we do, it will always be consensual and what we want. No one's expectations belong here with us.

"Okay, it's time for Mommy to get you ready for work. I have to get your bottom ready for your final plug."

"I like when you play with my bottom."

I tightened my fingers into her hips and rolled her on the thick shaft. I stroked my hands to her back and then pulled her down until she rested her weight on me. My body arched as she wrapped her lips around my nipple and rolled her tongue around it. I tenderly stroked her hair and watched as she suckled, her gaze on my face. She whimpered Mommy before she latched back on. I rocked her as I let her take her comfort from me.

The fingers of my free hand stroked her back, and I loved the way she completely relaxed. I'd let her nurse, and then I'd put her in the bath. I'd learned over the last few weeks that she loved to suck her thumb or my nipples when I laid her down for her nap. I'd gotten her a pacifier. She was learning more about being a little and testing things out to find what was right for her. Baby, toddler, or middle, she would always be my little love.

"My adorable, little love. You make me so proud." I lifted my head to brush a kiss to her forehead. Then I shifted until I could sit up, she wrapped her body around mine and released my nipple to rest her head on my shoulder. I felt her pout against my throat as I slipped free. I easily carried her to the bathroom, then sat her on the potty to ready her bath. She no longer tried to hold it like she had at the beginning.

I had the tub filling and turned to find her waiting for me to wipe her. When I reached her, I opened the box of wipes on the top of the tank, and she leaned forward so I could wipe between her thighs and her bottom before helping her to the tub. I let her play as I stripped off the harness, removed the dildo, and tossed the harness in the laundry basket. I cleaned the toy with gentle soap and set it aside to dry.

"Mommy?"

I looked in the mirror to find her watching me. "Yes, baby girl?"

"I know I asked before, but you're going to Thanksgiving with me, right?"

"Of course, I'm taking off the week so I can meet the parents of my little love."

I turned back to her to find her smiling at me shyly. For her, me meeting her parents was a big deal, and it was important to me too. Her parents needed to know that as far as I was concerned, she was it for me. If she agreed, I was going to keep her around for a long time. I'd fallen so easily for her, and as much as I wanted to tell her what she meant to me, for now I settled for showing her. I was respectful that being with a woman and being that woman's little and submissive was new.

She had all the time in the world to process, but soon I wanted to confess that I'd fallen in love with her. She was the best birthday present I'd ever received. I wasn't lying to her when I told her she was made for me. I approached the tub and stepped into it. I sat down, and she draped her thighs over mine while I grabbed the shampoo. She giggled as I washed her tangled hair, and she was so beautiful as she tipped her head back with her eyes closed and just relished my care. I gently and carefully stripped the soap from her silky curls.

I leaned forward and kissed the tip of her nose. "Little love, you are the best thing that ever happened to me, you know that, right?"

She didn't answer just hugged me, and I finished washing us both. I barely had her dressed and in the car in time enough to get her to work. I regretfully kissed her goodbye before I closed the door and watched until the car disappeared around the corner.

14

KATY

Our rental car pulled up in front of my parents' bungalow style house, and I smiled as I realized it still looked the same as it did when I moved out at eighteen. The only difference was my dad's truck was in the driveway. I was nervous, and my heart was pounding so hard I swore I could feel my chest pulsing with the rhythm.

"Little love, take a deep breath and slowly exhale. You're starting to panic." She laced our fingers.

I took comfort in her firm squeeze. Slowing my breathing took longer, and as much as I loved how she grounded me when I tended to panic, meeting the parents was a huge occasion. We'd talked on the phone. Lindy had several conversations with my mom, especially my dad. I just wanted them to like her; more than they'd liked the previous people I'd dated long enough for them to meet my parents. Bringing her there for a family holiday seemed important and a big step. I couldn't imagine not being with her, but I was also terrified about how my parents would react with the reality of meeting Lindy.

We got out of the car, and she grabbed our bag from the trunk. I stood on the curb waiting for her. She stepped up beside me and bent to sit our bag down.

"Baby girl, look at me."

She took my hands that I was currently wringing, and I focused on her warm, dark eyes.

"Your parents know we're coming. They know you're bringing a girlfriend to meet them. If at any point, you want to leave, I'll find us a hotel to stay in and change our tickets to head home. Your comfort and security mean everything to me, and you know that."

"I know, but it's different from phone calls. I want them to like you."

"This might sound rude, but the only person I want to like me is you. Them doing so would be a bonus. You know I'll do anything for you."

I nodded, and she dropped a kiss on my lips. She never denied or hid her affection for me. I'd met her friends, and she'd taken me with her to some business dinners with her clients and their significant others. She took so much pride in showing me off and telling everyone I was hers. She constantly touched me and made sure I was close.

"Let's go meet your parents so that you can relax. I don't like to see you upset."

She opened the gate and motioned me inside, I waited for her to join me, and she rested her hand on my lower back. A smile spread my lips wide as the front door opened, and my mom stepped outside. My dad, as always, was close on her heels.

"My baby is home." My mom ran to me, and I met her halfway.

I always missed home on some level, but I never realized how much until I arrived there. I needed to come home more than just holidays, but traveling wasn't easy especially when I was trying to save to buy my own place, and my dog walking clients depended on me. Mom held on tightly until she released me, and she cupped my face.

"I think you get more beautiful every time I see you."

I blushed, and it intensified when I heard Lindy chuckling behind me. I stepped back until I tucked myself under Lindy's arm. They were staring at Lindy. I didn't see disapproval or disgust. Although, their curiosity was nearly tangible as they studied us.

"Mom, Dad, I want to introduce you to Lindy Rubin, Lindy, my parents, Rebecca and James Campbell."

"It's a pleasure to meet you both. My little love has told me so much about you two."

She held out her hand, my mother gave it a quick shake, and my father gave a longer, firmer one. I could see he was measuring the woman I brought home to meet him. He seemed to come to some decision and released her hand.

"How was your trip?" he asked.

"It was great. I let my girl nap plenty on the plane. I know she was nervous about introducing us."

"Lindy."

She kissed my forehead and gave me a gentle squeeze.

"Remember your comfort is important to me. And your nervousness doesn't sit right with me. That will never change."

I suppressed a sigh at her Mommy voice. I loved it so much, almost more than her Mistress one that never failed to make me submit.

"Please, come in. I made some coffee, and then you two can get settled. Maybe have a nap before dinner. Several of Katy's friends have been stopping by and calling. I didn't know if she just wanted to spend time with just us this trip."

"If that's something Katy wants, then we'll make sure she has plenty of time to visit with everyone."

She motioned for my mother and me to precede her into the house where my dad held the door open. She followed us in, and I glanced back to find her setting our bag beside the door. She straightened and caught up with us in the kitchen. I covered my smile as she pulled out a chair for us, she didn't hesitate to pour first Mom and then me a cup of coffee from the carafe on the table. I sat still as I waited for her to make my coffee just the way I liked it, then placed a vanilla bean scone on a small plate beside my cup.

I was aware of how my parents observed us and that Lindy didn't change how she treated me simply because we were in my childhood home. I looked to the side and sensed that she was having a hard time not feeding me. She winked at me and nodded toward my drink and snack. She doctored her own coffee, and then she stretched her arm along the back of my chair. We waited silently as everyone settled in.

"Katy hasn't told us a lot about you, and our calls are usually brief. What is it you do for a living, Lindy?" Mom asked.

"I own a public relations firm, which means I just make people look really good when they make stupid mistakes."

"Don't let her downplay it. She's amazing at her job."

"Thank you, little love. It's just a lot of time in the public eye. Katy has attended some events with me, but I'm trying to keep her off the society page until she's more comfortable."

"Society page?" my dad asked.

"Yes, I attend a lot of high-profile events, and I'm also big on charity. When the donators have famous names, it has a tendency to draw the press. I'm well-known by association."

The interrogation continued, and she took it in stride,

answering each question honestly and patiently. She had nothing to hide, and the slight tension that surrounded my parents disappeared.

"Did you know my daughter was straight when you asked her out?" my mom asked.

I was about to protest, but Lindy's smooth voice cut me off.

"I was hopeful she was at least bisexual, but to be honest, even if our relationship never went past a platonic one, I would have been happy to have her in my life in any way I could. I will say that when she showed up at my door, I was extremely charmed."

"Me cussing out the man who stood me up was charming?"

"Everything about you is perfect, baby girl, you know that."

I caught my parents watching us with big smiles, and I loved that they seemed as taken with her as I was. I'd known even if they didn't like her that I wasn't going to stop dating her. Being with her was easy, and showing up at her place most nights was coming home. I hated spending nights alone at my place when I slept so much better in her arms.

"Have you met her parents yet?"

"No, Dad, they're in London, but every time they call her, I talk to them. They're flying in for Christmas."

"Yes, my mother has threatened me to be on my best behavior. She's waited a long time for me to find my one."

"So, you two are...serious?" my dad asked after taking a sip of his coffee.

I darted a glance in her direction and caught her watching me with that expression of complete adoration and love. She hadn't said the words, but she told me with every touch, kiss, and look in my direction that she loved me. During the *get to know* first meeting with my parents, she drew soothing circles on my upper arm with her thumb. Her side pressed completely to mine. She allowed no space between us.

"I can't speak for Katy, but as far as I'm concerned, I'm keeping her for however long she'll allow it. This is new for her, I'm the first woman she's dated, and while I've always been out, I know that she needs more time to come to grips with her first same-sex attraction. Whether we date for a few months or years, her well-being, mental and emotional, will always be dealt with open communication and no shame. It's important to me that she processes, and she's with me without any doubts clouding her feelings."

"Me and James have never been judgmental. People are free to live their lives how they want. And I respect you for allowing my daughter time to adjust, but from talking to her and the way she says your name"—mom glanced at dad—"I feel she's found the one she's waited for. I want you two to relax and enjoy your visit. You're always welcome."

I leaned heavier into Lindy's side as we had some more coffee, then I led her upstairs to my room. Mom had redecorated after I moved out, but it was still my room with all my things. Instead of a full-sized bed, a queen-sized one took up most of the room. I pivoted on my toes as the door softly clicked closed behind me. She approached me, and I backed up until the footboard stopped me, and she tossed our bag aside.

"Feeling better, little love?"

I nodded as she lowered her mouth to mine, but didn't kiss me. She retreated when I tried to capture her mouth with mine. I gasped as her hand slipped beneath my short dress, and she tugged the crotch of my panties to the side.

"Ready for your nap, baby girl?"

She parted my pussy lips and tweaked my clit. She worked it until I was panting and riding her fingers, and I was about to find my release when she stopped. I pouted as she covered me back up. I knew she did it because she liked knowing she'd made me wet—that I was ready for her.

"You know what you need for your nap, don't you?" Her voice was a husky whisper as I hopped onto the bed and scooted back. I kicked off my shoes. She slipped off her t-shirt to expose her unbound breasts, and from her motions, I knew she was toeing off her shoes. She climbed onto the bed and laid down on her side. I didn't even think about it, I just opened my mouth over her nipple and settled in. She lovingly stroked my hair, and I rolled my tongue tighter around her hard peak.

"You were so good for Mommy today. Let me take care of you. Trusted me. But now, my little needs to get her rest."

I loved being home to visit, but I missed our time to be us. My baths and my rocking chair, my sippy cups, and also my Mistress fucking me. Sometimes we even went days without sex, just Mommy and me, maybe my me-sized Teddy that I humped when Mommy left me alone to play. I loved our time together, but every touch turned me on, and I needed to release the tension. I didn't want to change the dynamics of our relationship— to me it was perfect. My body simply didn't understand that she, as my Mommy, didn't purposely arouse me.

My hand that conformed to the inner curve of her breast was moved to my lower belly, and she pulled my panties out.

Her touch didn't change, and not a word was exchanged. I rubbed myself off in frantic strokes, and I grunted around her nipple, increasing the suction. The pressure in my belly built until I broke, and I moaned long and low. I never stopped suckling at her nipple, and I snuffled as I pushed closer.

"That's my good girl, take a nap."

She hadn't chastised just placed my hand between my thighs and allowed me what I needed. I kept my hand between my thighs, rubbing my release through my pubic curls as I slowly drifted to sleep with her Mommy voice in my ear, telling me a story, and her soft lips caressing my forehead.

15

LINDY

I squeezed her soft tummy and nipped at the side of her neck. Her giggle made me smile as we stood at one of the tall tables at the back of the bar waiting for a group of her high school friends to arrive.

"You know I could lift the back of your skirt right now, and no one would know you were riding my fingers." I gruffly chuckled at her high-pitched moan, and she rubbed her plump ass against me. We were spending our last night visiting her parents by letting my baby girl reconnect with her friends. She was uncomfortable having sex in her childhood room, but I told her every night what I was going to do to her when we got home as she got herself off. Just listening to her rub one out while I watched was enough for me.

"Quit being mean."

"How am I being mean, little love?"

"You know I feel awkward having sex with my parents down the hall."

"And have I pressured you into doing anything?" She shook her head in answer, and her cheek rubbed against mine. "We'll make up for all of it when we get home."

I knew she was still adjusting to being with me and that a good portion of our relationship wasn't about sex, that I was just as happy when I got to be her Mommy as I was when she submitted to me as her Mistress. And being there with her parents, I still indulged in my nurturing and caretaker aspects. Fed her and even gave her a few baths, put her down for her naps. I respected her wish to go no further than the dirty talk and masturbation.

"Katy," several voices mixed, and I lifted my head to find four women and two men approaching.

I let her go, and I grinned as I watched my baby girl greet her friends.

"You must be Lindy. I'm Levi." A big man with a lopsided smile stretched his arm across the table.

I shook his hand and then introduced myself to a tall, super lean man called Stretch. He rolled his eyes as he explained he got the name when he shot up from five-foot to six-five.

"Lindy Rubin."

"Katy kinda shocked us. We did a search—"

I laughed as I reached for my beer. Search engines were the bane of my existence. My little love almost didn't go out with me because of the society page. I loved my job, and the press was part of that. "Yeah, my baby girl did that too. I think she almost didn't go out with me."

She nudged me with her hip as she came up beside me, and I draped my arm around her. "You know that's not true. Cecile made sure I didn't say no."

"I still owe her for that one."

I shook hands with the ladies as she introduced them to me. I ordered a round of drinks as they went to claim a pool table. It was a Sunday night, and it was still early, so the place wasn't packed. I swiped a tray and easily carried the bottles and glasses across the room.

"Interviewing for another job?"

I dropped a kiss on her lips as I passed her. "No, my days of slinging booze are over. It definitely doesn't pay my bills like it used to."

"The days when you weren't high maintenance with your brownstone and thousand-dollar suits."

"Don't be mean, baby girl. And you love me in my custom suits."

"I really, really, really do." She fluttered her long lashes at me, and I couldn't even fuss at her for her brattiness.

Everyone laughed and then thanked me as they took their drinks. We racked up, joked through several games of pool, and more drinks, and greasy bar food.

"Man, okay, I miss bar food, though." I took a bite of pizza as she leaned back between my thighs. I wrapped my arm around her thick waist.

"How did you get into public relations?" Holly, a pretty, petite brunette asked.

"I take after my mom, biggest con artist to ever be born, and I inherited her talent to make anyone look good. To be honest, it's not all scandals and shit. It's just my job to maintain a company or person's image. A minority of my clients make a pain of themselves. It takes a lot of trust when you're privy to everyone's secrets.

"Now, I want all the embarrassing stories on my little love here."

Katy protested loudly through every story that included everything from streaking to her first night drunk—which made me plan to get my girl tipsy when I found out any alcohol made her hot and prone to taking her clothes off. My baby girl needed to strip for me one night.

As the evening progressed, I realized that her friends didn't make a big deal about my gender or that I was the first for her. She was happy and free, laughing and smiling as they shared memories, and I made a mental note to plan to bring her home more often. I knew what it was like to miss my parents, but for me, it was a way of life. My parents traveled, and we spent months, sometimes a year apart. My friends I'd made overseas were just as busy as I was, and we exchanged the occasional email to catch up. The friends at home were the same. Busy lives and demanding careers made sustaining connections hard. I wanted to make sure she never lost contact with the people who made her look like she did at that moment.

Last call came quicker than we expected, and I paid the tab as everyone protested. We all waited outside for the cars we requested from our ride-share apps. My baby girl exchanged hugs and goodbyes with her friends and promises to visit again soon. I offered to put them up if they ever wanted to come to Ivy Harbor. I opened the door for the ladies and helped them inside while the guys hopped into their car.

We were left alone with a few more minutes to wait.

"Did you have fun?"

"So much fun, thank you for this. My parents and friends loved you."

"I'm glad. I wanted them to like me because I knew it made you happy."

She twined her arms around my waist and rested her weight against me. "You always want to make me happy, Lindy."

"I do because when you're happy, so am I. Being your Mommy and your Mistress takes precedence. And once I arrange it, hire more staff, my nights and weekends will be for you unless an emergency comes up."

"I told you, you don't have to change everything for me."

"That's the thing." I raised my hands to cup her face and made sure she focused on me. "I don't *have* to do anything. I want to because I made a promise to myself on my birthday I was going to make changes. Then you showed up at my door, and it all fell into place." I dropped a kiss to the slight curve of her lips. Saw the happiness in her beautiful, pale eyes. "Didn't I tell you, you were the best birthday present I ever received."

"That kiss after our first date, it scared me, but I wanted more. It felt...right."

"And it should always feel right."

I was about to kiss her when the car pulled up, and I helped her inside. As soon as I slid in beside her, she cuddled to my side, and we started the trip across town to her parents' place. She nestled her face into the curve of my neck, and I bit my lip to hide my moan as she lightly sucked at my throat. Her left hand stroking over the flat plane of my stomach, and her thumb nudged the lower curve of my unrestrained breast. I eased my hand into the waistband of her jeans and cupped her soft, lush hip and then around to her belly just above her soft big girl curls. I wanted to bury my hand between her dimpled thighs and drive my fingers deep. Her hips shifted restlessly on the seat beside mine, and she licked up to my ear. Her teeth tugged at my earlobe.

We had our flight late afternoon, and when we returned to our place, I'd give her all the love and attention she'd missed out on the past four days. She needed her little time. I knew how much she found comfort in her little girl clothes and her sippy cup, her freedom to play with her toys as I watched her from our rocking chair until she was ready for her story and nap. But I also knew the blissed-out expression as I bound her slowly in soft ropes to be used however I saw fit. Every time I whispered in her ear how my slutty girl craved her Mistress' cock, and she only became wetter.

She was the dichotomy of slut and innocent that I'd always yearned for, and she blossomed as she accepted her roles—the freedom of her complete and willing submission. When we pulled up to the curb, I removed my hand from her pants. I paid and tipped, told him goodnight and to have a safe one.

We got out and made our way up the walkway.

"Mommy?"

"Yes, little love?" I glanced down, and her gaze glittered in the glow of the porch light.

"I wish we were home."

"I do too, but soon. You can have your room and your toys. Then you can come to your Mistress' bed after your nap."

She shifted her body and rose onto her toes, her mouth almost touching mine. "Can I always be your little girl and your sub?"

"I love you, Katy, and I want to keep you for a very long time."

She gasped, and I kissed her before she could answer. I snuck her inside and up to her room. I helped her use the potty and dressed her for bed in her favorite gown for her naps. When I tucked her in all safe and sound, I kissed her and told her I'd be right back after I got myself ready for bed.

She smiled so sweetly and shyly as she snuggled under the covers, her tiny teddy bear cuddled to her chest. Her eyes drifted shut as I watched her a few minutes longer, my lips twitched as she slipped her thumb into her mouth. She always wanted to be mine, and I'd make sure she never regretted belonging to me.

16

KATY

I danced on my toes as I finished my shift, and I giggled every time Cecile nudged me. Lindy had to work, but she gave me her credit card and a list of places to visit to buy myself some things. Although, she was going to try to take a break to meet me. There was a store that catered to Mommy and Daddy Doms and their littles. She wanted me to research and see if I'd like to regress younger. We'd talked over dinner the night before and made a list of things I'd like to try. I didn't mind when she helped me potty when I was little, but I didn't know if I'd be comfortable in diapers or training pants.

Most of my excitement was about visiting a place where I could be little outside our home. I was completely comfortable in my sub and little roles. I no longer second-guessed myself. She made sure Mommy or Mistress were always ready to meet my needs. She'd awakened me that morning and dressed me in a cute onesie, let me watch cartoons with my teddy while she made breakfast. Mornings were always heavy with Mommy and little girl time, especially if I spent the night which recently had increased in frequency.

I quickly removed my drawer and rushed to the back to take care of the paperwork.

"Slow down, Katy, what has you so excited?"

"Lindy and I are going shopping. She's taking a break."

"Naughty shopping?"

"No, new clothes and stuff. She said I needed more things to keep at her place." That was partially true. I even had a few things at my place to wear when we were apart. She'd taken to asking for a picture at bedtime to make sure I was properly dressed and prepared for bed. She even read me a story over the phone on nights she had to work late. I preferred when she did it in person while she rocked me and let me nurse. I craved the connection when it was time to sleep. My thumb and pacifier didn't have the same effect.

"Getting serious."

"Yes, but I don't think we're at the moving in stage yet. For right now, I think she just wants me to make her place mine when I do stay over. I think I'm there most nights anyway, or she comes over before work for breakfast. She told me she loved me when we went to my parents for Thanksgiving." I whispered the last part like it was a secret.

"Oh my god, what did you say?"

"Nothing, she kissed me and took me inside before I could. She's so worried about if I'm happy and wants me to have no doubts about what we have when I say it. Which I appreciate. It's just so easy being with her. Natural. I asked if I could always be hers, and that's when she said she loved me and wanted to keep me."

"And to think it all happened over a mixed-up address."

"I know, she said I was her best birthday present."

"I swear you lucked out, a beautiful, successful, loving,

and attentive girlfriend. Whose only goal in life is to make you happy. Maybe it was meant to be, fate brought you to her house and on her birthday no less. Well, hurry up and finish so you can go spend time with Lindy."

I nodded and finished adding everything up, stowed the drawer, and escaped outside after pulling on my winter coat. It was always bitterly cold during winter as the wind came off the harbor. Christmas would be there before I knew it, and I needed to get Lindy something special. I just didn't know what yet.

After pulling out my phone, I slipped on my backpack and sent Lindy a text that I was on my way to the store. I opened the map app to type in the address and realized it was about a fifteen-minute walk away. A notification opened at the top of my screen with her reply.

Lindy: Calling Gary now. Be there in thirty.

I sent a quick message to tell her okay and that I missed her. I went over the list she'd sent to my phone. She'd be there for shopping for little me, but the sex shop I'd be visiting alone. It wasn't the first time I'd gone to one, but vibrators and all were a single girl's best friend, but this was the only time I'd gone to pick out toys that my Mistress would use on me, or I'd use while she watched.

When we'd gone to my parents, I'd found her talking to me as I got off sexy, and I wanted to do it again so she could watch freely in our bed or wherever in our home. Her brownstone was home, and my apartment was just that. It turned into a place to keep my things and nothing more.

I stopped in front of a cute shop and opened the door. I walked into what I assumed was little heaven.

"Good afternoon, welcome to Little's Place, I'm Freda."

"I'm Katy, um, my, um..." I didn't know what to say.

"Mommy, Daddy, or Parents?"

"Mommy."

"Very good, is she meeting you here?"

"Yes, she was leaving work but wanted me to look around. We made a list of things I wanted to try." I held up my phone with the list we shared, and I let my gaze move around the store. A rocking horse caught my attention, and it was sized for me.

"Perfect, I can help you until she gets here if you want. Are you new to being a little?"

"Yes, first time, Mommy said I was still learning and finding my way. She said my needs are toddler to pre-school."

"Fun age, all the toys and baths. Daddy swears I get as dirty as possible outside just so he has to give me a bath."

Freda and I talked. I asked her questions about items, and she didn't hesitate to answer some more personal questions. She said sometimes littles needed to stick together. She even handed me a card for a little playgroup that took place at different houses every week. Her Daddy ran a club where littles could play together, and parents could socialize. Lindy had never mentioned something like that, but I wondered if she was waiting until I was more secure as my little before she did.

"Little love, are you behaving?"

I turned to find Lindy looking elegant and beautiful as always. She was smiling at me, and as she approached, she looked into the cart. Clothes, dresses, nightgowns, and ruffled underwear, I'd even thrown in some cloth diapers and training pants. I couldn't say I didn't like it if I didn't try.

"Yes, Mommy."

"Seems you've found some stuff you liked."

"She's been asking questions too. I'm Freda."

"Lindy. I thought she'd like some private time to look over her options before I showed up. We've been talking about regression lately."

"Well, she's very informed for a first time little. I was commenting that she has an amazing Mommy."

"And I hope she thinks so."

"Well, I'll leave you two to finish your shopping. Just a suggestion, she's barely resisting trying out the rocking horse."

Lindy chuckled as I blushed, and then we were left alone in the aisle.

"Were you having fun, baby girl?"

I nodded as she brushed a kiss to my forehead. "A lot. She gave me a bunch of cards and flyers about playgroups and stuff."

"Is that something you'd like to do, play with other littles?"

"I think I would. Maybe get to know people like me who I can bond with."

"And I think that's a great idea. I had it on my list of things to talk to you about at some point, but didn't know if you wanted to keep your little side just between us."

"I'm not going to tell the world, but spending time with other littles could be fun."

"Well, then we'll look at schedules and plan some play-dates for you."

"Thank you."

"You don't have to thank me. Making you happy makes me happy."

We spent two hours going through each aisle. I looked to her for permission every time I threw something in the cart. My eyes widened as Freda gave the total, and I started to protest, but Lindy used her Mommy voice, and I was done for. I nearly danced when she requested the rocking horse and a huge dollhouse to be delivered with the rest of the stuff. Freda said the delivery guy would be back in an hour, and she'd send our purchases right over.

We parted outside the door, and I headed home to wait for the delivery. Lindy told me she'd be a bit late, but I told her I could wash my new clothes, cups, pacifiers, and take my stuff to my room. She told me to play as long as I wanted, and she'd make dinner when she got home. I gave her a kiss and ordered a car to take me to the brownstone.

I couldn't help smiling as I sat in the back of the car, thinking about my new things, Lindy and the upcoming adventures. I'd never felt so free and loved, and it had everything to do with Lindy, my Mommy and Domme. She made everything easy and right. I couldn't wait for the months and years ahead, because to me, it wasn't if we were together—I always wanted to be only hers.

17

LINDY

"Little love, are you home?" I called out as I walked inside the house a few hours early, shut the door, and then set my briefcase on the floor beside the foyer table. I loosened my tie as my dress shoes tapped on the hardwood floors. She wasn't living with me full-time yet. Although, she was here more than she was at her apartment. As much as I wanted to ask her to move in, we just weren't there.

Christmas approached, and I was still searching for the perfect present for my baby girl. She wasn't in the kitchen or living room. She'd texted me that she was on her way, but maybe she had to stop at the store first. I jogged up the stairs to the third floor, my steps quieted by the thick carpet, and I froze as I stepped into my bedroom. My baby girl was on her hands and knees in the middle of the bed. The base of her plug exposed, and she was working her clit with the tip of one of her vibes.

Her huge teddy bear under her, and I saw her rubbing her breasts on its soft fur. Her moans and shrieks were muffled where her face was buried in the plush toy. She was so focused on her pleasure that she didn't know I was there. I knew if she'd sensed me, she would've turned around and begged me to take over. I quickly stripped myself of my shoes and clothes, eased open the drawer, and put on my harness.

I bit my lip to hide a groan as she eased her plug out, and then the long, slim vibrator replaced it. She fucked her stretched bottom and lowered her pussy onto her bear. I retrieved the lube and a condom from the drawer of our toys. I smoothed the latex down the length and carried the small bottle to the bed. Taking the plug was one thing, but I wanted to make sure I didn't hurt her. As soon as my knees sunk into the bed, she jerked her panicked gaze to me over her shoulder. She removed the vibe and started to turn over.

Before she had a chance to hide from me, I surged forward and pressed my hips and pelvis to her ass.

"Is this what my baby girl does when she's waiting for her Mommy and Domme to get home?" I smoothed my slicked hands over her ass and up her back, and then around to her breasts. The shaggy bear teased the backs of my hands while her velvety warm skin did my palms.

Her only answer was a nod as she lifted her arm, and her hand sunk in my hair as I nudged her wrinkled hole with the balls of my strap-on. I impatiently lubed her hole and my length until I shifted, placed the head to her opening and pushed. She tensed beneath me.

"Hurts."

"Easy, baby girl. I'm gonna take such good care of you." I straightened, retreated, added more lube, and fucked her in small increments until she was reaching back to spread her cheeks. "You should see how stretched your bottom is for your Mistress and Mommy."

"Fuck me, M—Mistress, please, I need it." She whined

and pouted at me over her shoulder as she wrapped her arms around her bear, arched her ass upward, and prepared.

I used her how I saw fit, fucked and owned her, stamped my ownership on her in handprints and love bites. She'd scream for more, then beg me to stop in the next breath. I knew what she needed, and as I brutally reamed her ass for the first time, I turned on the vibe, placing it on her clit. My stomach drew in tight, the straps between my thighs slick with my need, and my pussy clenched. I frantically turned on the bullet vibe inserted in my strap on and worked to get us both off. Her sobs met my grunts, and I looked down to stare at her red, swollen rim. The vibrations were too much for the both of us, and I came seconds before I noticed her entire body tensed and arched, I jerked from her and turned her on her side. Raised her right leg to brace her thigh on my stomach, ripped off the condom, and then thrust into her pussy.

Her nails dug painfully into my side as I drove her toward a second, and third release, by the time the last one hit, she was limp and shaking. My muscles screamed from the exertion. I fell to the side, our legs still tangled as I turned off the bullet and laid there trying to catch my breath. I looked at her to find her staring wide-eyed at the ceiling, her breathing ragged, and a small smile curving her lips.

My baby girl's hips were still jerking where my thigh pressed to her soaked slit. I caressed her leg where it rested across my lower belly, and when I felt her skin start to prickle with the cold, I dragged a blanket from the foot of the bed to cover us.

"Come here, little love."

I loved her even more when she weakly dragged herself

to stretch out beside me, and her head came to rest on my shoulder.

"I'm going to be home waiting every day."

I chuckled at her awe-tinged voice and lifted my head to brush my mouth to hers. "And I will voice no complaints."

"You really like it when I masturbate."

"I do, nothing sexier than my baby girl taking control of her pleasure. Is that why you have me wash your bear every other day?" I knew it was. I'd caught her a few times as she'd rode her bear, and I'd watched her a few minutes before leaving her to finish. Little Katy just needed alone time to take care of her needs, and unless she asked me, I wouldn't presume to help my baby girl get off.

She nodded and cuddled closer. "I know Mommy doesn't mean to arouse me, but when you leave the room, I hump my teddy."

"And I've told you, our bodies reacted to being touched and caressed. I get excited too when I bathe you and let you suckle my nipples to go to sleep. When it's Mommy and Katy, I just want to give you all the love and nurturing that you need. I crave the intimacy of being with you without needing to fuck you. That doesn't mean that one day Mommy and Katy time doesn't involve some grownup touching. We're still learning what we both need from each other."

She stroked her fingers over my stomach beneath the light blanket.

"And until we're happy with our dynamic, you can play with your toys however you want. Your teddy is your favorite comfort item."

"I love you, Lindy. I've wanted to say it for months, but I was scared at first. I'm in my thirties, and while I've said it to people before, what we have is so much more than that."

"And you know I love you. I've shown you in every way possible and also said it. I knew you'd say it one day, but I needed you to be sure of me, your Mommy and Mistress. This is our life. When you move in, this will be twenty-four-seven. That's a lot to accept. And when you're ready, I want to move you in permanently."

"And I want that, too."

"But you need more time. I told you, little love, the trust and commitment we're going to need doesn't happen in a few months, sometimes it takes years, but I'm patient because I know that one day it'll happen. And until I get the firm fully staffed, I'd love for you to be waiting for me when I get home, but I don't like you having to be here alone and waiting."

"And I love you more for that. Can your little love have control to make you feel as good as you make me?"

"I'm always yours, Katy."

She lifted until she straddled my hips, and I stretched as she kissed her way down the center of my body. And I didn't hesitate to spread my thighs for her. I closed my eyes at the first slow lick over my clit. I shuddered at the gentle suckling, almost like she did to my nipples before she went to sleep. I lifted my head, and my gaze met hers as my little love gave me head. Wanton and intense, messy and out of control and perfect.

"Fuck," I cursed as my eyes closed as she slid two fingers deep and didn't stop until I screamed and shattered with the strong suck of her lips latched onto my clit. I savored her control and need, the way she took command of my pleasure.

When I was nothing more than a relaxed, quivering mess, she kissed her way back up. Her mouth came down on mine, and I cleaned her lips of my release. Her wet pussy rutting against my lower stomach until we both calmed.

"Mine?"

"Always, little love. I waited way too long to find you to let you go."

Lazy kisses and conversation turned into a night in bed, and us making dinner naked at midnight. Laughing and being silly as we fed each other. It hadn't been about work taking precedence that kept me from finding the love of my life, no, it was fate and one night when she finally delivered who I needed to my door.

EPILOGUE

KATY

I cuddled under my blanket, sucking my thumb as Mommy read to me. She was combing her fingers through my hair. Today I'd needed to just be. I wanted cuddles and time in our rocking chair. For a year, we took every moment we could, but it hadn't happened overnight. Finally, she'd assembled a team she trusted, and this was our first weekend alone in three months. Her voice tapered off as she read *The End*.

"Turn over."

As I turned over, my thumb slipped from my mouth, and I found her studying me. "Do you know what today is, little love?"

"Our anniversary."

"Yes, it is." She scooted downward and rolled to face me.

I couldn't help it when my eyes closed as she stroked my cheek. Every touch still made me feel as if I was the only one who existed for her—her entire focus. Compartmental-izing her life had taken its toll on her. I hadn't demanded any more than she could give me. I knew she'd do every-thing within her power to keep me.

"A year ago, you showed up on my doorstep and became my everything in a few rambling sentences. What would you like for your present?"

I opened my eyes to look at her. I loved that indulgent tilt of her mouth and knew I could ask for anything. "Um, whatever you got me is perfect."

"Who said I got you anything?" she asked.

"Are you saying—" I paused as she started to pick at the tiny pearl buttons of my nightgown. "That you didn't get me a present for a year of dating you? I think that would at least warrant a reward."

"Ouch, my baby to brat in the span of minutes."

She pushed me onto my back and parted the fabric, exposing my breasts and belly, my panties with teddies on them. I whimpered as she removed her presence. I didn't protest or call her back. She hadn't gone far, just to dig into the nightstand. When she turned back to me, her fingertips stroked along the delicate chain circling my throat with just two charms, an L and a K. She'd given me the chain our first night she became my Mistress. The charms came on my birthday. I found myself touching them several times a day to remind myself that we belonged to each other.

I was about to ask what she was thinking when an envelope was placed on my chest, and I picked it up.

"What's this?"

"Your present, well, part of it anyway."

I slipped my finger beneath the flap and tore the seal. I pulled out two round trip tickets to Paris. The trip was for two-weeks. "You can't take—"

"Little love, I've taken off a month starting tonight. I arranged the time off with your boss, but not for another two weeks."

I threw myself at her and straddled her hips as she

allowed me to roll on top of her. I sat up and stared at the tickets. "A whole month, just us?"

"Well, I'll have my phone and laptop for emergencies, but unless it's something they absolutely can't handle without me, everyone agreed to leave us alone."

"This is too much, Lindy." I protested, but whatever other excuses I was going to give ended as a ring appeared.

"You wear my collar, my ownership, and our contract seals that you're mine. This ring is the final step. I want to marry you. You were destined to be mine as much as I was made for you. You're my baby girl, my little love, and my perfect partner. We don't have to run to the altar, not tomorrow, or even a year from now."

"What if I want to get married in Paris?" I asked as I took the ring from her hands. It could've been a larger diamond, but it fit me.

"Then I'll have to buy more tickets. Your parents would end me if they weren't at the wedding."

"I think a part of me fell in love with you the moment you took care of me. You didn't have to. I was no one but a crazy woman on your doorstep." She cupped my face and pulled me down until our mouths almost touched.

"You were so much more than that. Will you marry me? You have to answer me with complete honesty before I slip that band on. If you can say you have no doubts."

She pushed my limits but always demanded my consent.

"I never doubted you. You've always made me feel special. Even with work, you never failed to say goodnight or call me in the morning to tell me to have a good day. I want nothing more than to marry you. Even if you hadn't proposed, I wasn't going anywhere. My trust and commitment has nothing to do with you putting a ring on my finger."

I moaned as her fingertips dug into my hips.

"Maybe I want my ring on your finger so everyone knows you're mine."

"I don't think you have to worry about that. Everyone knows I'm taken."

I gasped as she sat up and hugged me tight.

"And I will make sure you're always happy to be taken. So will you marry me and be my wife and little the rest of our lives together?"

"Yes."

I didn't hesitate, not a single doubt existed. I wanted to be right here, today, tomorrow, and fifty years from now. I always wanted to be her Little Love.

ABOUT THE AUTHOR

Siobhan Smile is an author of happily ever afters with a twist. They features characters of all sizes, shapes, sexualities, gender identities, and races. Reading a Siobhan Smile book lets you escape for a few hours whether that is to an alien world or a contemporary setting, you'll find something outside the norm. Writing books for Siobhan is more than simply telling a story, it's a way for everyone to see themselves get a HEA.